HER SEARCHING HEART

A proposal of marriage from Robert, whom she does not love, brings Valerie face to face with a frightening question — is she incapable of falling in love? She rejects Robert and flees to the tranquillity of Cornwall, hoping to find the answer; but when she meets Bruce and his motherless young daughter Mandy, she discovers new and disturbing emotions deep in her heart — and finds the answer to her question . . .

PHYLLIS MALLET

HER SEARCHING HEART

Complete and Unabridged

LINFORD
Leicester

First published in Great Britain in 1989

First Linford Edition
published 2014

A catalogue record for this book is available
from the British Library.

ISBN 978–1–4448–1864–2

Published by
F. A. Thorpe (Publishing)
Anstey, Leicestershire

Set by Words & Graphics Ltd.
Anstey, Leicestershire
Printed and bound in Great Britain by
T. J. International Ltd., Padstow, Cornwall

This book is printed on acid-free paper

1

Valerie lay awake through the small hours after tossing and turning for most of the night, wondering if she'd ever get another good night's sleep! The nearby church clock chimed four, and then, after what seemed an eternity, she heard it strike five. Frustration seized her and she sat up in bed, hands clenched, mind filled with conflict. Did she or didn't she want to marry Robert?

Slipping out of bed, she pulled on a dressing-gown and padded down the stairs to the lounge, where she switched on the gas fire and huddled in a corner of the settee, blue eyes staring into space.

At the beginning she'd believed herself to be captivated by Robert, but last evening, when he'd proposed, she'd been seized by a cold certainty that she was not in love at all and marriage

1

would be a great mistake.

Not that there was anything wrong with Robert! He was a man in a million — rich, handsome, cultured — a prize that any sensible young woman would jump at. But Valerie knew in her heart that she didn't love him, and the certainty had grown stronger during this sleepless night.

A sigh escaped her. This uncertainty was intolerable. She felt like a bird trapped in a cage. But she was also sorry for Robert! He obviously thought a great deal of her, and it would hurt him badly when she refused him. But she couldn't even contemplate marriage, and should have made that clear the minute he proposed.

The door of the lounge opened and her father peered in. He stifled a yawn and came into the room, his expression filled with concern.

'What's wrong, Val?' he demanded. 'I heard you come down. Not feeling ill, are you?'

'No, Dad.' She smiled wanly. 'Robert

proposed to me last evening!'

'Good! I've been wondering when he would pop the question. I like Robert. He's a good lad.'

'But I don't want to marry him!' Valerie shook her head.

Jim Kenton opened his mouth to respond, but something in Valerie's expression stopped him. He saw the agony of indecision in her eyes, and sighed heavily. There was no job in the big garage he owned that he could not do, but trying to understand his 24-year-old daughter was beyond him, and he knew it.

'This is one of the times I wish your mother was still alive,' he said, sitting down at her side and putting a protective arm around her slender shoulders. 'She would have known how to handle this! Are you sure it isn't just nerves, Val? Robert's a nice fellow.'

'No, Dad, I'm positive. I'm not in love with Robert enough to want to marry him. I like him, of course, and we've been very close friends. But I shrink from the thought of marrying him.'

'Well, you should know your own mind,' he observed. 'And if you feel so strongly against marriage then it would be foolish to let this situation develop further. Speak to Robert first thing in the morning. Then you can have a good think about it and decide what you really want to do.'

She looked at him with a glimmer of relief in her eyes. 'I'll do that, Dad,' she said firmly. 'I can't stand this indecision. It's like a nightmare.'

He patted her shoulder. 'Don't worry about it! That's the worst thing you could do. Robert will understand.' He paused. 'Would you like me to have a word with him?'

'No thanks. I'll talk to him.' She sighed, relieved now the decision had been made. 'Would you like something to drink?'

'No thanks.' He smiled. 'I'll get back to bed.'

She nodded, and went back to bed

with a firm decision in her mind. Now she was more relaxed, and drifted into slumber. Later, upon awakening, she was horrified to discover that the time was almost eight o'clock. She sprang out of bed and hastily began to prepare for the day.

Jim Kenton was in the kitchen, frying eggs and bacon, and he raised an eyebrow in silent invitation.

'No thanks, Dad.' She shook her head and opened the fridge door. 'I'll just have my usual.'

'What have you decided about Robert?' he asked.

'I'll talk to him this morning.' She compressed her lips. 'I'm not looking forward to it, but he has to be told. And I suppose it will mean the end of a very good friendship.' She paused and then said slowly. 'What I'd really like to do is get away from it all for a time!'

'There's the holiday bungalow in Cornwall that I bought last year,' he offered. 'You haven't been down that way yet, and I think the solitude will do you good. Take as long as you need! I can run things here.'

'I'll think about it.' She shook some cereal into a bowl and poured milk on top. 'Don't forget that you've got Mr Tropwell coming in at nine-thirty this morning for a test drive.'

'The garage could run itself,' he commented. 'But I wish you luck with Robert. He's a good lad, if overly determined.'

Valerie silently agreed. She wasn't looking forward to the confrontation. She'd no desire to hurt Robert. But if she did not call a halt now he'd be hurt a great deal more later.

After breakfast she walked to the main road that ran through the dormitory village of Little Barnsford and stood by the war memorial. Five minutes later, Robert's red Rover appeared and pulled into the lay-by. His smiling face greeted her as she opened the front passenger door.

'Valerie, bright and beautiful as usual,' he said in a rich tone. He was darkly handsome, smartly dressed, a senior partner in a firm of chartered accountants established by his late father.

'Robert, I must talk seriously to you this morning,' she began.

'Jump in,' he invited. 'I can tell that you've accepted my proposal. Now we can begin to plan the wedding.'

She slid into the seat and closed the door. Taking a deep breath, she began to speak as he did, and, instead of stopping as usual, she continued to talk until he frowned and fell silent.

'Please listen to me,' she begged. 'I am not accepting your proposal, Robert. I can't marry you!'

'What's wrong?' He frowned. 'You look as if you didn't get any sleep last night.'

'There's nothing wrong! It's just that I can't consider marriage to you.'

He shook his head, as if impatient with her attitude. 'If you want more time in which to think it over,' he said vaguely, waving a hand.

7

'No.' She spoke unhappily. 'Obviously, I don't care enough to want to marry you or I'd be in raptures about your proposal. Instead, I'm not very happy because my rejection will mean the end of a very good friendship.'

'I love you, Valerie,' he said quietly, 'and I assumed that you loved me! But if there are any doubts in your mind then of course you must not agree to my proposal yet.'

She kept her gaze on him while he spoke and saw shock in his expression. His face had turned pale. She shook her head miserably.

'I'm sorry, Robert. I guess I'm just not the marrying kind!'

He glanced at his watch and a sigh escaped him. Then he shook his head. 'Look, I have to be going. I'll come round this evening and we'll talk it out. I'm sure we'll be able to set it right.'

'I won't be at home this evening.' She reached the decision even as she spoke. 'I need a complete break. I must get away from everyone and everything.'

'But you can't go off just like that! Val, you're overwrought. Wait until we've had an opportunity to talk things over.' He paused, noting her manner, and then nodded. 'All right, go away for a short break. I'm sure you will see everything in a different light when you come back.'

'I feel like never coming back,' she retorted. 'You must accept that no matter what I do, I'm not going to change my mind about us, Robert. I just don't love you!'

He was shocked and hurt, and she felt sorry for him. But she had to be cruel to be kind.

'Please don't feel too badly,' she pleaded. 'It's better that we settle this now rather than later. I'm sure you will eventually find someone who will return your love, and you deserve the best, Robert.'

He sighed, fingers clenching and unclenching around the steering-wheel. Valerie watched him, and could imagine what was passing through his mind.

'What about all our friends?' he asked harshly. 'What do we say to them?' He shook his head. 'What will they say?'

'That should be the least of our considerations,' she retorted.

She shook her head sadly and got out of the car. Robert leaned sideways and closed the door, then drove away slowly. Valerie watched the car until it disappeared around a bend, aware of relief slowly filling her mind. Then she exhaled sharply and turned resolutely to walk the short distance to her father's garage.

The mechanics had not yet arrived but Jim was in the office, and she knew that she could not face the day at work. Her father looked up at her entrance, noted her expression, and threw down his pen with a sigh.

'You look dreadful, Val,' he observed. 'Are you all right?'

'I feel better now,' she responded.

'So you've told him!' He nodded. 'Good. Now take my advice and drop out of circulation for a time.' He pulled open a drawer, rummaged inside, and produced a bunch of keys. 'Here are the keys to the bungalow in Cornwall. Go and spend a few days there. In fact, you can take as long as you like.'

An intangible emotion stirred in her breast and she picked up the keys, trying to reach a decision.

'Go on,' Jim urged. 'The nice weather is almost upon us. It will be beautiful in Cornwall now. What do you say?'

'Yes!' A sigh of relief escaped her as she spoke. 'But only on one condition.'

'What's that?'

'You won't tell anyone where I'm going.'

'It's a deal. Now you'd better get moving, and don't forget to send me a postcard.'

Two hours later, Valerie was driving to Cornwall, her spirits higher than they'd been for a very long time. The farther she drove from home the more relieved she became, and by the middle of the afternoon she was nearing

Cornwall, certain that she'd made the right decision.

An hour later, she drove through St Austell on her way to Truro, where she had a cup of tea in the cathedral tea-room before driving on to Ryn-haven. It was almost five when she drew up at the bungalow perched high on a cliff overlooking the sea, and her brown eyes sparkled with appreciation as she gazed around at the exquisite scenery.

The bungalow was large, she noted, as she parked the car and took her cases and provisions inside. The power was on, and she plugged in the fridge and prepared to settle in.

When the water had heated, she showered, revelling in the soaking to which she subjected herself. Being completely alone gave her soul balm after the anxiety and worry of the past days. But she was eager to explore her surroundings, and locked the bungalow and followed a path that led along the cliff-top.

The sun was getting low in the sky

and the shadows were lengthening. The sea was rough against the foot of the cliffs, a stiff breeze blowing onshore. She stood gazing around appreciatively, completely alone in a vast, picturesque wilderness that had her already captivated.

She was tempted to descend a cliff path that led into a beautiful cove, but darkness would soon fall. Tomorrow was another day, and she meant to be out at first light to take full advantage of this unexpected holiday . . .

That night she slept peacefully for the first time in weeks, and was ready to go exploring as the sun appeared on the eastern horizon. She dressed warmly and soon found the footpath leading down into the cove. The tide was out, she noticed, as she descended the path, which was steep in some places and almost unscalable in others.

Then she reached surprisingly firm sand, noting that she hardly left footprints as she ran towards the water's edge.

There were masses of seaweed! Rock pools littered the cove, the water in them crystal clear. She spent a rapturous hour poking around, collecting shells and pretty stones, and all thoughts of the past vanished from her mind as if they'd never been. She felt at peace with the world, until a low, menacing growl disturbed her and she jumped up, to be further startled by the sight of a large Alsatian dog which showed its teeth in a frightening snarl.

Valerie caught her breath, and then spoke soothingly to the dog, which crouched and fixed her with unblinking eyes. It growled again, quivering with hostility, and she was nervous, for it looked as if it would attack at any moment.

'We could be friends, boy!' she said, and the sound of her voice caused the dog to cock an ear, but its menace never wavered. It crouched even lower, its hackles standing on end.

'Rajah!' A man's voice echoed in the distance, and the dog immediately

14

stood up. 'Rajah! Stay, boy!' There was a pause, during which Valerie did not move a muscle. Then, 'Sit, Rajah!'

The dog sat down, still looking dangerous, but did not relax. Valerie suddenly realised that she was holding her breath, and released it in a long sigh. She dared not move, and time seemed to stand still, until she heard the thud of feet on the firm sand. Risking a glance over her shoulder she saw a man approaching swiftly, his face hard.

'What the devil are you doing here?' he demanded, halting at her side.

'Is that your dog?' she countered, angry now the immediate danger was over.

'It is, and you're very fortunate that I was close when he came upon you.'

'He's dangerous, and should be kept on a lead!' Valerie disliked his tone and manner. 'I didn't do a thing to antagonise him, and he was ready to pounce on me!'

'I'm not surprised! His job is to protect my property. You're a foolish woman to take such risks.'

'How was I to know the dog was here?' she demanded, becoming incensed.

'What are you doing here?'

'Nothing that warranted an attack by any dog!' She clenched her hands.

'You're trespassing! This cove is strictly private, and Rajah knows that no-one should be down here!'

'Then why haven't you put up warning notices to alert unwary people? It's against the law to let a dangerous animal roam at large without proper warning and safeguards.'

'It's also against the law to trespass, and I do have signs up at either end of the cove.'

'Well, I didn't come into the cove from either end. There's a path towards the centre which I used, and I certainly didn't see any sign or I wouldn't have descended.'

He turned his head to glance in the direction she indicated, and she took the opportunity to study his profile. He was dark-haired, about 28, she guessed, and rather handsome, although his good looks were somewhat marred by his anger.

'The path you mention leads to the bungalow. Is that where you're staying?'

'The bungalow belongs to my father. I arrived last evening. Why isn't there a warning notice at the top of the path?'

'There was one! But I expect one of the locals pulled it down and threw it over the cliff. It often happens. That's why Rajah is on patrol here.'

'And what if a child had wandered down here?' Valerie was breathing heavily. 'It could have been badly savaged, or worse.'

'Local children know about Rajah,' he said gruffly, and she realised that she had put him on the defensive.

'That's not good enough! If I had brought a child with me and it wandered down here alone, what do you suppose would have happened to it? You'd better do something about that path!' She made as if to turn away, but halted when the dog growled deep

17

in its throat. She sighed. 'If you'll put the dog under control, I'll leave,' she said pointedly.

'Stay, Rajah,' he ordered, and the dog relaxed.

Valerie glared at him before turning away, and then tried to depart with dignity, which was not possible on the sand. But she did not look back and kept moving until she reached the path and had ascended several feet. Then she risked a look down, and frowned when she failed to see the man or the dog. She sighed heavily as her anger began to drain away.

Well, she thought, that kind of confrontation was too much for one's nerves! The dog had only been doing its job, she knew. But the man had been something else! Apart from his brusqueness, he had been as hostile as the dog! She made her way up the path, filled with mixed emotions, aware that she needed a strong cup of tea to settle her nerves. And she vowed that she would never again set foot in the cove!

2

By the time she reached the bungalow, Valerie's nerves had resettled. She made a cup of tea, and sat on the sofa to drink it. Reaching for the telephone, she dialled the number of her father's garage, and a sigh escaped her as she glanced at her watch to see that the morning was still young. She could imagine her father just getting into the office, and here she was, already back from a long invigorating walk.

'Good morning, Kenton's Garage,' Jim said in her ear, and she shrugged herself free from a sense of unreality, aware that leaving home was the best thing she could have done.

'Hello, Dad. It's good to hear your voice,' she replied.

'Val! Hey, I was wondering when you would get around to calling me. How are you doing? Not wishing you were home already, are you?'

'No.' She chuckled. 'Your advice to get away from it all was good, as usual. This morning all my problems seem a million miles away. Are you managing to run the office without me?'

He laughed, and she pictured his face. 'Don't worry about a thing,' he said firmly. 'Everything is under control. But is there anything you need? Are you happy on your own?'

'Yes, thanks. I wouldn't want it any other way at the moment.'

'Robert called to see me yesterday evening.' His voice was casual.

'You didn't give him my whereabouts, did you?'

'Certainly not! Mind you, he all but pestered the life out of me for the information, but I told him you needed time in which to think things over and he said you could have as long as you need.'

'I don't need to think it over! I'm not in love with Robert, and that's all there is to it.'

'All right. That's fine. So enjoy your holiday and confirm your decision when you return. It's as simple as that, Val.'

'Yes. Of course. Thanks, Dad, for being so understanding.'

'That's what fathers are for, isn't it?' He chuckled. 'Give yourself plenty of time and it will work out, you'll see. Enjoy yourself, and let me know if there's anything you need.'

'I will, and thanks again.'

'Fine. I'll be thinking of you, Val. Goodbye now.'

'Goodbye, Dad. I'll call you again, soon.'

There was a soft smile on her lips when she hung up, and she drank her tea thoughtfully. The sun was shining through the front windows, and the silence was so intense that it hurt her ears. For a moment she thought of Robert, and was saddened. But she arose and crossed to the window to gaze at the exquisite scenery. Then she experienced an urge to go out and

21

further explore the locality, it was all so beautiful.

But she avoided the cove, and her lips pulled into a thin line as she recalled her encounter with the dog and the man. She followed the cliffs, marvelling at the blueness of the sky and the serenity of the sea as she walked briskly in the fresh air. The solitude was perfect, and her thoughts faded away to nothing under the spell of Cornwall at its best.

Her mother had been born in Cornwall, and Valerie remembered the little snippets of information that had come to her at her mother's knee. Now she was seeing it all, and her heart swelled and her thoughts settled back into perspective.

The morning passed quickly, and at noon she returned to the bungalow for a snack. The fresh air had put an edge on her appetite, and, after eating, despite the ache in her legs, she obeyed the restlessness of her soul and set out to explore the cliffs in the opposite direction. Her thoughts returned to Robert but by the time she reached a mansion set atop the cliffs, she was sure she'd made the right decision.

The sound of a car on the driveway ahead disturbed the deep silence, and she frowned when a vehicle came towards her. Then she recognised the driver as the man who had been in the cove with the dog, and shrank back into the cover of a tree as the car drew abreast.

The man seemed a bit grim-faced as he passed by, but he did not see her, for which she was thankful, and when he had disappeared into the distance she continued her walk, skirting the house, which, she discovered upon drawing nearer, was a hotel. She regained the cliff top beyond the hotel and went on, but paused with a frown when she became aware of a dog barking, for there was something in the sound that warned of an emergency. She approached the edge of the cliff and peered down.

There was a winding path leading to the beach far below, and Valerie saw an Alsatian dog standing on a wide ledge about halfway down. It was barking frenziedly while gazing up at the cliff top, and she recognised it as the one that had been in the cove. Not wanting to be seen, she turned away immediately, but the dog must have spotted her for it came racing up the path, barking even more furiously.

Valerie feared a repetition of that earlier incident, but the next moment the dog was at her heels, grasping the hem of her dress and pulling her to a halt. She drew a deep breath as it tried to tug her in the direction from which it came. Then it released her, ran back to the path, paused, and turned to stare at her. It was now uncannily silent. Valerie tensed as comprehension flooded her. Then she began to follow. The dog turned immediately and began to descend the path, with Valerie following as quickly as she dared.

When they reached the shelf, Valerie

saw a young girl, aged about eight, lying motionless on a ledge off to the left. They were about fifty feet above the beach, and Valerie's blood froze as she brushed by the dog and hurriedly bent over the girl, who was lying on her back with her eyes closed. At first Valerie thought the child was unconscious, but, as she touched her shoulder, the youngster opened her eyes and stared up at Valerie.

'Are you all right?' Valerie demanded, squatting by the girl's side. 'Do you need any help?'

'I turned dizzy,' the girl said. 'I'm not supposed to come down here alone, but it's such a nice day. My daddy should have brought me but he was called away on business.' She paused and subjected Valerie to a close scrutiny. 'Would you take me the rest of the way?'

'Certainly, if your dog won't object.' Valerie helped the child to her feet, studying her keenly. She was petite, dark-haired and brown-eyed, with rather pale features. Studying the young face, Valerie experienced a pang of misgiving. 'Perhaps we'd better take you home,' she mused. 'You don't look very well.'

'I'm all right, really I am! I was ill, but I'm better now.'

Valerie smiled at the worldliness in the girl's tone, but she was struck by the pathos that showed in her dark eyes.

'I'm sorry to hear that you've been ill,' she remarked.

'I wasn't really ill!' The girl shook her head to emphasise the point. 'Doctor Carter said it was only natural after such a trauma.' She said no more, and Valerie wondered what she meant.

'Where do you live?' she asked. 'I think I'd better see you home. If you're not supposed to be on the cliffs alone, then it's foolish to disobey orders. They were obviously made with your best interests at heart. What's your name?'

'Mandy. Mandy Stirling. I live in the hotel on the cliffs. But I don't know you. Do you live around here?'

'No. I live near London. I'm Valerie

Kenton, and I'm pleased to meet you, Mandy.' Valerie smiled and held out her hand and Mandy responded shyly. 'Let's take it very carefully up here, shall we? Do you still feel dizzy?'

'Not now, thank you. It's worn off. But I would like to go down to the beach, and if you took me it would be all right, wouldn't it? I shan't be alone.'

'Haven't you been warned not to go off with strangers?' Valerie demanded.

'Yes. But I can tell you're all right.'

'Take my word for it,' Valerie said seriously. 'You can't tell if anyone is all right these days.' She looked into the young face, and smiled at the disappointment which was showing plainly in the girlish expression. She felt a sudden yearning for company herself, and tightened her grasp upon Mandy's hand. 'I'll tell you what we can do,' she suggested. 'Let's go and ask if I can take you on the beach.'

'Would you?' Mandy's brown eyes gleamed.

Valerie nodded, and the Alsatian,

which had been lying patiently with its nose on its paws, arose and bounded up the path ahead of them.

'Are you on holiday?' Mandy inquired.

'Yes. For a week or so.' Valerie informed her. 'You're lucky, you know,' she added, 'living here in Cornwall with your home right on top of the cliffs. It must be a wonderful sight in winter, watching the storms.'

'If we hadn't lived here my mother would still be alive,' Mandy said with a seriousness that was not in keeping with her tender years.

A pang stabbed Valerie as she glanced at the frowning young face. 'Your mother is dead?' she asked.

Mandy glanced up at her and nodded. 'She fell off the cliff the winter before last. That's why I like to walk in the cove. That's where they found her body when the tide went out.'

Valerie shook her head wordlessly, and for some moments they continued the ascent in silence. The dog was standing at the top of the cliff now, staring down at them, and Valerie recalled the way it had acted toward her in the cove earlier. But then she had been an intruder and now she was a friend.

They paused to catch their breath when they reached the top of the path, and Valerie looked down at the beach.

'I can understand why you were told not to go down there alone,' she commented. 'It's very steep, and could be quite dangerous.'

They walked along the path and turned in at a wide gateway that led to the hotel. Valerie looked around with interest, noting that the place was well maintained. She pictured the man who had accosted her on the beach, who was obviously Mandy's father. Perhaps the fact that he had lost his wife fairly recently accounted for his brusque manner, she thought, and studied the Alsatian which was never far from Mandy's side.

'What's your dog's name?' she asked.

'He's Rajah.' Mandy dropped to one

knee. 'Rajah, here, boy.' The dog approached quickly, wagging its tail, and licked Mandy's hand. 'Now say hello to Valerie,' the girl said, and Valerie bent to pat the dog.

'Hello, Rajah,' she said, and was rewarded with a lick on the hand.

They went on and entered the hotel. Valerie remained in the lobby while Mandy went into the office, to emerge a moment later with a tall, middle-aged woman following her.

'Mandy, how many times do you have to be told not to go near the cliffs when you're out alone?' the woman was rebuking sharply.

'It was all right, Miss Harper,' the girl replied, moving to Valerie's side. 'Valerie was there, and she would have taken me on the beach but she said we had to let someone know first.'

'Quite right, too,' Miss Harper retorted, turning to look at Valerie. 'Thank you for bringing Mandy home, Miss . . . '

'I'm Valerie Kenton.' Valerie explained

30

how she had come across Mandy. 'I'm on holiday,' she volunteered, 'and I'd like Mandy's company for the afternoon, if that's all right with you.'

'She's a good girl, generally,' Miss Harper said. 'And if you don't mind burdening yourself with a child!' She glanced at Mandy. 'Go and wash your face and hands, dear, and then you can go with Miss Kenton.' She waited until Mandy had departed, then sighed. 'Poor girl!' she said in a softer tone. 'She's quite a problem these days. Since her mother died she's become very withdrawn, and has no interest in anything except getting down into that cove where it happened.'

'She told me something of her mother,' Valerie said.

'She did? Well that's something! One of her problems is that she won't talk about her mother to anyone, not even her father.' Miss Harper glanced down at Rajah, who was sitting patiently at Valerie's side. 'That dog seems to have taken a liking to you! Perhaps there's going to be a breakthrough in Mandy's condition after all! We've been very worried about her.'

'She's a likeable child,' Valerie observed. 'And you needn't worry about her being in my company. I'll take very good care of her. My father owns the holiday bungalow on the cliffs about a mile from here.'

'Ah yes!' Miss Harper nodded. 'I thought your name was familiar. Your father must be Jim Kenton! He was a frequent visitor here last year when he came to buy the bungalow.' She smiled, an undefinable expresson touching her eyes. 'I got to know him quite well in the time he was here.'

Mandy returned at that moment, eager to go down to the beach, and they took their leave of Miss Harper. Rajah bounded out of the hotel as if aware of their plans, and Valerie took hold of Mandy's hand . . .

When they reached the beach, Rajah ran off at top speed, making for a cluster of jagged rocks, and Mandy stared after the dog, looking as if she wanted to follow.

'That's where they found my mother, in those rocks,' she said in a strained tone, and turned in the opposite direction. 'Let's go this way. Rajah will come back when he sees we're not following him.'

Valerie warmed to the girl as they walked along the shore. They searched for shells and white stones, and found starfish and other small marine creatures in the rock pools. Time passed quickly because they seemed to lose all sense of it, running hither and thither, throwing stones for Rajah, who dashed fearlessly into the sea. At first, Mandy was withdrawn, Valerie noticed, face pale and eyes listless. But by degrees she became less inhibited, and after two hours, was running around, shouting, calling, and bubbling with laughter like any normal child.

It was with great reluctance that Valerie, upon checking her watch, decided that it was time to start back to the hotel.

'I don't want to go back yet,' Mandy protested, dark eyes gleaming. 'I'm having a lovely time.'

Valerie smiled indulgently. 'I must confess that I've quite enjoyed this afternoon,' she replied, and smiled as Mandy came and slipped a hand in hers. 'You've got some colour in your cheeks now, Mandy. You need to get out into the fresh air more often, you know.'

'I haven't been going out much, but I enjoyed this afternoon. Do you think we could go out again?'

'I don't see why not. You could show me around and we'd both enjoy it. But you'll have to talk to your daddy about it. He may not like the idea of you going with a stranger. Daddies have to be very careful, you know.'

'Daddy's all right!' Mandy spoke confidently. 'He'll be glad if you take me out because he never gets time to himself. I think he works very hard to take his mind off Mummy.'

They started back along the shore, carrying their finds, and Mandy chatted in lively fashion. Rajah ran on ahead, exploring every nook and cranny, startling gulls that were feeding and chasing them when they flew away. Mandy's laughter echoed along the deserted shore.

Valerie was tired when they reached the cliff top, and they paused, glancing back at the beach and the sea. Mandy heaved a big sigh.

'I'm so glad you came here for a holiday, Valerie,' she observed. 'If you hadn't, I wouldn't have had so much fun.'

'Yes.' Valerie nodded as they went into the hotel. 'It's been a happy time for both of us.'

'Daddy will be surprised when he comes home and finds that I've been happy,' Mandy said slowly. 'He's been trying hard to get me to enjoy myself. But he hasn't any spare time for me.'

'Some daddies have to work very hard,' Valerie remarked, 'and your daddy must be one of them.'

'Miss Harper says he should spend more time with me, especially now.' A plaintive note crept into Mandy's voice, and Valerie shook her head as she glanced down at the wistful face turned appealingly toward her. She smiled and placed a hand upon the girl's slim shoulder.

'Don't worry too much about it,' she advised. 'I'm sure it will all come right.'

They entered the hotel lobby and Valerie looked around cautiously for Mandy's father.

Miss Harper emerged from the office, smiling when she saw them. 'Ah, there you are,' she said pleasantly. 'Do you have to leave now, Miss Kenton? I'm sure Mandy would like you to have tea with her.'

'Please stay, Valerie,' Mandy pleaded, and Valerie agreed without hesitation.

Miss Harper gazed at Mandy as if unable to believe the change that had come over the girl, and Mandy smiled self-consciously.

'I'll take Valerie to my room, and she can freshen up before we have tea. Will you stay until Daddy comes home, Valerie?'

'I'll stay and have tea with you,' Valerie replied, 'but after that I ought to leave. If your daddy has gone out on business he may be late coming back.'

'I'll talk to your daddy,' Miss Harper said. 'Take care of Miss Kenton now, Mandy, and bring her down to the dining-room when you're ready.'

'My hands got dirty but Valerie's didn't seem to,' Mandy observed lightly.

Miss Harper exchanged a glance with Valerie, who was conscious of a warm emotion in her breast as she accompanied Mandy to the stairs. She glanced over her shoulder when Rajah did not follow, and Mandy nodded.

'Rajah knows he's not allowed upstairs,' she said. 'He'll wait in the office until we come down.'

Valerie nodded, and they went up to Mandy's room, which was at the very top of the building. Its wide window gave a perfect view of the cove and the sea. Valerie stood for some moments, gazing seawards, enraptured by the view. Mandy went into the bathroom, and when she reappeared she looked as if she had scrubbed herself. Her face shone, and her eyes were animated. She was like a different child.

When they went to the dining-room a waitress appeared and Mandy ordered something to eat. Valerie would have been content with a cup of tea, but Mandy insisted that they share a Cornish cream-tea. There was silence while they ate, but then Mandy began to chatter, and Miss Harper paused in the doorway and listened for some moments before approaching the table.

'Is this really Mandy Stirling?' she demanded in mock surprise. 'I've never seen her so lively! The spring sunshine must be doing her a power of good. Or could it be the company she found herself this afternoon? If that's it, then I hope we're going to see a lot more of you around here, Miss Kenton.'

'Please call me Valerie!' Valerie smiled. 'I must say that I found Mandy quite refreshing, and I'd like to take her out again.' She glanced at her watch. 'But I really ought to be running along now. I hadn't planned to stay away from the bungalow so long.'

Mandy's expression changed, and Valerie reached across the table to touch her hand.

'I'll come and see you again,' she promised.

'Tomorrow?' Mandy demanded.

'Certainly tomorrow.' Valerie nodded. 'I have nothing planned for the morning.'

'I'll walk to the gate with you.' Mandy slid away from the table.

Valerie walked with the girl, and Rajah appeared from nowhere to shadow them. When they reached the cliff path, Mandy squeezed Valerie's hand.

'I'm so glad you came here on holiday,' she said softly. 'Will you be my friend until you go back to London?'

'Of course I will!' Valerie was touched by the girl's manner. She bent and impulsively kissed her cheek. 'I'll come and see you in the morning.'

'Please do!' Mandy clung to her for a moment, then stepped back reluctantly. 'Goodbye, Valerie.'

'Not goodbye,' Valerie countered, smiling. 'Until tomorrow.'

As she departed along the cliff path she glanced backward several times, to see Mandy still at the gate, waving vigorously. Valerie waved in return, and when she finally moved out of sight of the hotel, she sighed and shook her head.

Mandy was an entrancing girl, she told herself, and was thankful that she had found her on the cliff path before a mishap occurred. She felt strangely attracted to the girl, and realised it was because Mandy was still suffering from the untimely loss of her mother. And being in the child's company had taken her mind off her own problems, with the result that her sense of frustration had lifted completely. She was feeling much more relaxed.

She returned to the bungalow with a heart that was lighter than when she had set out earlier. Robert was now safely consigned to the background, she discovered, and the awareness filled her with relief. She had unconsciously climbed out of a rut, and realised that a few more days like today would enable her to come to terms with reality. She hummed light-heartedly as she let herself into the bungalow. Now she could appreciate the wisdom of her father's advice to get away from all things familiar.

3

After taking a bath, Valerie felt refreshed and comfortable, and settled down to relax. There were several books on a shelf in the long living-room, so she selected a novel, and tried to get interested in it. However, she soon found her thoughts turned to Mandy. She couldn't eradicate Mandy's face from her mind. There was something about the girl that touched Valerie's heart. She had seemed so alone, in a world of her own.

There was a knock at the door, and opening it she found Mandy's father standing on the step, with a sheepish smile upon his rather handsome face.

'Hello,' he greeted, and lunged for Rajah as the dog darted past him to spring at Valerie. She staggered under the impact, and Rajah licked her face. 'Well I never!' he exclaimed. 'I've been hearing glowing tales about you ever since I returned to the hotel this evening, but I didn't think Rajah would take to you like this. Did you put a spell on my daughter and my dog, Miss Kenton?' he asked, laughing at Rajah's antics.

Valerie smiled and shook her head. 'It was nothing, really,' she replied. 'I merely showed Mandy some friendliness, and gave her the attention she seems to need.'

'Yes.' He nodded ruefully. 'I realise I haven't been giving Mandy enough time, but I have to work out my own salvation, and that's been almost too much to handle.'

'I wasn't refering to your circumstances,' Valerie hastened to say. 'I was merely making an observation. Perhaps I'm being a bit presumptious . . . '

'Not at all.' He spoke gravely. 'Sometimes it's easier for an outsider to see where the root of the trouble lies. I've been very worried about Mandy for a long time now, and the doctor can't really tell me how she ought to be handled. But I returned home about an hour ago and saw a great change in her. I couldn't believe it at first, until Miss Harper filled in the details. Mandy has come out of her shell for the first time today, and you are her one topic of conversation.' He paused, his smile again somewhat sheepish.

Valerie smiled, but before she could speak he held up a hand.

'I feel awkward facing you after the way I acted in the cove,' he said. 'But, really, I was more concerned with what might have happened to you if Rajah hadn't kept himself in check.'

Valerie smiled, feeling slightly embarrassed. 'That's all right,' she said. 'Would you care to come in for a cup of tea? I was about to make one,' she added.

'Thank you.' He nodded. 'I'd like that. I came straight over after seeing Mandy to bed, and I haven't eaten anything since I left home this afternoon.'

'That's far too long to go without,' she said sympathetically, stepping aside for him to enter. 'I saw you leaving the hotel, as a matter of fact, and that was hours ago.'

He sighed as he crossed the threshold. 'Yes. Everyone tells me I'm working too hard. The trouble is, it has to be done.' He grasped Rajah's collar. 'Do you mind if Rajah comes in?'

'Not at all. I like dogs.' She led the way into the lounge and offered him a seat.

'Let me introduce myself,' he said, pausing in the act of sitting down. 'I'm Bruce Stirling.'

She smiled. 'And I'm Valerie Kenton, as, no doubt, you already know. We meet under friendlier circumstances today.'

'I'm glad. I felt terrible about that incident in the cove, and I intended looking you up to apologise. Thank goodness you're not going to hold that encounter against me.' He paused, smiling disarmingly. 'Or are you?'

She shook her head emphatically. 'I'm not the type to hold a grudge, Mr Stirling.'

'And then there was today, and you coming to Mandy's rescue. I dread to think what might have happened to Mandy if you hadn't been on the spot to go to her assistance.'

'It really wasn't as bad as it sounded.' Valerie related the incident, making a point of Rajah's part. Bruce nodded and bent to pat the dog.

'He's one in a million,' he asserted. 'If only he had been with my wife on the night . . . ' He broke off, shaking his head, and Valerie excused herself and went into the kitchen. When she emerged moments later, with two cups of tea on a tray, she found Bruce glancing through her book.

'Do you read much?' he enquired, setting down the book and taking a cup of tea from her. He looked up into her eyes, and she felt the force of his gaze, the intent look in his eyes.

'As a rule I never get time to read,'

she admitted. 'But I'm here alone on holiday, and reading is a marvellous way to relax after spending all day seeing the sights.'

'Miss Harper suggested that I come and talk with you because Mandy is over the moon about going out with you tomorrow. But, as you're on holiday, I'm sure the last thing you want is a child around.'

'I don't mind in the least,' she began.

'I've been promising for ages to take Mandy out somewhere,' he continued, 'and tomorrow will be the first day I've been clear of business for as long as I can remember. So I think I'll take her to Adamporth, and that will let you out of any promise you made to her.'

'I'm glad you can find the time to take her out,' Valerie responded. 'But she was no trouble to me, and I'd be glad of her company some other time. She told me she's missing you, and I fancy your company would really help her get over the loss of her mother.'

He nodded. 'Fine. I have no objections to Mandy going out with you. In fact, it's rather kind of you to take pity on her. You are on holiday!' He paused, then asked, 'How long are you staying here?'

She shrugged and sat down in an easy chair opposite. 'I haven't really decided. Two weeks, perhaps.'

'Is it an early holiday, or have you been ill?'

She smiled. 'It's neither, actually. A personal problem brought me away from home. I don't usually take a holiday this early in the year.'

'I see.' He smiled. 'I'm not prying, but if you're staying any length of time then feel free to use the amenities at the hotel as you wish. I remember your father from last year, when he came down to buy this place. He spent a couple of nights at the hotel, and became quite friendly with our Miss Harper.'

'Yes.' Valerie nodded. 'Miss Harper mentioned it this afternoon.' She paused. 'It's very kind of you to give me the run of the hotel.'

'Not at all! You're a friend of Mandy's, and any friend of my daughter is a friend of mine, as the saying goes.'

'Thank you.' Valerie leaned back and sipped her tea. She gazed at him, fascinated by his good looks. But there was a brightness in his eyes which warned that he was labouring under an emotional burden, and she felt sympathy for him and his daughter. He drank his tea with evident enjoyment and then stood up.

'Thank you for the tea,' he commented, and Rajah arose and padded to the door. 'I expect we shall be seeing you at the hotel.' He glanced at Rajah and then shook his head wonderingly. 'I can't get over the way that dog has accepted you,' he mused. 'And his approval is better than any testimonial. Rajah doesn't take to just anyone.'

Valerie smiled as she saw him to the door. He turned when he was outside, and took her hand, shaking it rather formally.

'Thank you again for what you did this afternoon,' he said. 'And please do come to the hotel when you feel like it. You may get rather lonely after you've been here a day or two. Solitude is all very well, but you can have too much of a good thing, you know.'

'I'll bear that in mind,' she promised, smiling, and remained on the doorstep to watch his departure.

When he had gone and she was again seated in the lounge, she felt strangely unsettled. Acting upon impulse, she lifted the telephone receiver and called her father.

'Hello, Dad.' she greeted. 'How are you?'

'Missing you,' he responded. 'How have you spent your day?'

'Do you mean to tell me that you don't already know?' she countered.

'How would I know?' He sounded completely mystified.

'You have a friend hereabouts, I've

learned, and I was wondering if you had asked her to keep an eye on me.' Valerie chuckled. 'Miss Harper at the hotel along the cliffs from here, Dad. Don't tell me you've forgotten all about her! She spoke quite highly of you this afternoon.'

'Ah!' It was his turn to chuckle. 'To tell you the truth, I had forgotten about her, but please don't tell her that, Val! Give her my regards when you see her again.' He paused, and then said, 'So you've been to the hotel.'

Valerie explained briefly about her meeting with Mandy.

'What do you think of Bruce Stirling?' Jim asked.

'Poor man! I heard that his wife died in a cliff accident about two years ago. What a terrible business! His daughter, Mandy, is such a sweet child. And she misses her mother so very much.'

'Yes. I remember them very well. He's a worker, is Bruce, and if he isn't remarried to Ruth Ordway then he's a fortunate man. I never saw a woman who made her intentions more obvious than Ruth, and she is one very determined female.'

Valerie listened in silence, her face marred by a frown. So there was a woman somewhere in Bruce's life! Her frown deepened as she wondered why that fact should be so disturbing.

'I'm more concerned about Mandy,' she said softly.

'I see. Well, my advice is not to get involved with the family through Mandy,' Jim said. 'That way could lead to untold heartache, Val.'

She chuckled, but the sound did not seem too convincing in her own ears. 'I'm not going to get involved with anyone, for whatever reason,' she retorted. 'Good night, Dad. I'll call you sometime tomorrow. And don't worry about me. I'm perfectly happy here.'

She was thoughful after hanging up, and tried to dismiss all thoughts of Mandy and Bruce from her mind. Even in bed that night she had difficulty in finding sleep, and tossed and turned for quite a while before eventually entering the blissful realms of slumber . . .

At breakfast next morning, Valerie was contemplating the day that stretched before her when there was a frantic scratching sound at the door. Frowning, she went to open the door, and Rajah came bounding in, tail wagging furiously.

'Hello, Rajah,' she said cheerfully, patting him. 'What brings you here at this time of the morning?' She half-hoped that Bruce was outside.

'I brought him, Valerie,' Mandy called, and Valerie looked up to see the girl in the background.

Mandy's face was pale, etched with disappointment, and Valerie felt her heart go out to the child as she went forward to take hold of her hand. Something had clearly upset the child.

'What's wrong?' Valerie demanded.

'It's Daddy!' Mandy was close to tears, and Valerie experienced an impulse to clasp the child to her breast. 'He told me this morning that he can't take me to Adamporth as he promised.

An important business meeting has come up unexpectedly. And I was so looking forward to going with him!'

'Well, that's nothing to get upset about,' Valerie said soothingly. 'If he can't take you out today then he'll certainly be able to another time, so if you're set on going to Adamporth today then why don't we go together? I've heard a lot about the place, but I don't even know where it is!'

'It's easy to find,' Mandy said eagerly. 'Would you take me, Valerie? I could go somewhere else with Daddy, when he does find the time to take me out. I'd love to go with you.'

'I'd love to take you,' Valerie responded. 'Have you had breakfast yet?'

'I was so disappointed about Daddy that I couldn't eat anything,' Mandy admitted.

'Well, you've got nothing to be disappointed about now so come in and help me eat my breakfast,' Valerie retorted.

Mandy chuckled as they sat down to

breakfast, and very soon regained the vivaciousness she had displayed the day before. She ate everything that Valerie placed before her, and helped clear the table and wash and dry the dishes afterwards.

When they were ready to leave, Mandy opened the door and Rajah departed at top speed to chase the birds.

'We'd better go back to the hotel first,' Valerie decided. 'Rajah has to be taken home, and we must let Miss Harper know that I'm going to take you out for the day.'

'Daddy will be gone by the time we get there,' Mandy said.

'We'd better go in my car or we'll have to walk back to get it, and we need to make an early start.'

The girl chattered animatedly all the way to the hotel, and Valerie noted her change of manner and was surprised by it. Miss Harper was thankful that Valerie was able to take Mandy for the day, and made the girl go and wash her face and hands and change into a clean dress. She took the opportunity to speak to Valerie once they were alone.

'Mr Stirling felt certain that you would take Mandy out when she told you that he couldn't manage it today. I told him that he ought to get his life into perspective, and give more time to his only daughter. I don't know what could be more important than Mandy's mental wellbeing, and he's jeopardising that by his misjudged priorities.'

'I suppose there are some things in business that just cannot be postponed,' Valerie said. 'But Mandy is not unhappy about the situation now. And she'll be quite all right with me.'

'She will, I have no doubt.' Miss Harper reached into a pocket and produced a 10-pound note. 'Mr Stirling told me to give you this, and if your expenses prove to be higher then you must let him know.'

Valerie smiled. 'That's kind of him.' She paused, and then smiled. 'I called my father last evening, to let him know how I'm getting along, and he asked to be remembered to you.'

Miss Harper smiled. 'I thought he'd forgotten me,' she responded clasping her hands together. 'How's he keeping?'

'He's fine! He may be coming down for a holiday later in the year.'

'I'll look forward to seeing him again,' Miss Harper acknowledged.

Mandy returned, bubbling with excitement, and Miss Harper shook her head wonderingly when she noted the degree of the girl's exuberance.

'I can only hope that your change of attitude will be permanent, Mandy,' she observed. 'You don't look like the same girl now.'

'I feel better now,' Mandy replied cheerfully.

Miss Harper smiled and glanced at Valerie. 'It's your influence,' she said, her eyes twinkling. 'If you only knew how depressed Mandy has been! We couldn't do anything with her. Even the doctor was worried. But you seem to have taken her out of it with no effort.

How did you do it, Valerie? It's amazing the way she's taken to you.'

'I didn't do anything,' Valerie protested. 'Perhaps Mandy was coming out of it naturally, and my appearance on the scene was purely coincidental.' She looked at Mandy, who came forward and grasped her hand.

'Come on, Valerie, let's be going,' she said, and Miss Harper smiled as she returned to the office.

Valerie led the way out to her car, and paused as she opened the door to settle Mandy in.

She closed the door and went around the car to slide in behind the wheel. Adjusting the girl's seat belt, she buckled her own and then looked at Mandy. 'I don't know where Adamporth is,' she reminded. 'So you'll have to be the guide until we get there. Which way do I drive when we reach the main road? I do hope you can keep me right.'

Mandy thought for a moment, then nodded. 'It's all right,' she said confidently. 'I do know the way. I just had to remember it, because I haven't been there for such a long time.'

She was silent until the car was moving through the gateway, and then glanced at Valerie, who was surprised to see tears in her eyes.

'Is anything wrong, Mandy?' she asked gently.

'I don't know,' Mandy replied, trying to smile. 'I don't feel sad! It's my eyes, not me! They're flooding, that's all.'

'I expect your emotions are trying to straighten themselves out,' Valerie said. 'Just sit quietly and it will pass, I'm sure. Are you certain you still want to go out for the day?'

'Oh yes!' Mandy smiled through her tears. 'I'm looking forward to it. It's not my fault if my eyes water.'

Valerie chuckled and drove on, and after a few moments Mandy's tears had evaporated and she was once again staring around and trying hard to enjoy herself. She instinctively decided that if it was within her power to help then she would do everything that was humanly possible to bring happiness back to Mandy.

Mandy gave directions for the trip to Adamporth, although Valerie could quite easily have found her way with the help of the signposts. But the pleasure in the girl's eyes was worth all the extra effort required, and, when they eventually pulled into the large car-park just outside the tiny Cornish fishing village, Mandy was once more brimming over with pleasure and happiness. There was no more sign of tears.

Valerie looked around with great interest, for she'd heard much about this part of the country, although it was the first time she had managed to visit. She was pleasantly surprised to discover that Adamporth itself was apparently untouched by time and progress.

'Would you like an ice-cream, Mandy?' Valerie enquired.

'Only if you'll have one, too,' the girl replied instantly.

They bought ices and stood gazing

out at the sun-dappled sea. Mandy managed to get ice-cream on her nose, and Valerie snapped her with the camera before she could wipe it off.

Later they boarded a small motor-boat that was crewed by two men dressed as pirates, and the craft was flying the skull and crossbones. The pirate captain, complete with black eye-patch, let Mandy steer the boat, much to her delight, and, when they returned to the stone pier, she clutched impulsively at Valerie's arm.

'I've never had so much fun,' she declared. 'I wish Daddy was here with us, but I'm glad I didn't come alone with him. It wouldn't have been half as much fun.'

'If you let him know you prefer my company he may never take you out again,' Valerie warned.

'I wish you lived in Cornwall,' Mandy said, and Valerie noticed that her eyes had lost their sparkle.

But she soon regained her high spirits when they went into a shop and Valerie presented her with a big, cuddly teddy bear.

They had lunch in a smart, cliff-top restaurant, and sat for some time just admiring the view. The afternoon was spent browsing around the shops, and, to round off the day, they rode up to the car-park outside the village in a special horse-drawn carriage.

Mandy was not content until she had stroked the horse's nose, and then they went to the car and prepared to drive back to the hotel. Mandy almost fell asleep, such was her exhaustion, but the dreamy expression on her face indicated just how much she had enjoyed the day . . .

4

When they arrived at the hotel, Mandy
stirred and sat up to look around.
Valerie was absorbed with the operation
of parking the car, and glanced quickly
at Mandy when the girl gave a shriek,
and began to jump about in her seat in
obvious excitement.

'It's Daddy,' she cried, pointing to a
car that was edging into a parking place
nearby. 'He's home early! Now I can
tell him about our day.'

Mandy shot out of the car and ran to
the other car, calling to her father.
Valerie alighted and waited by her door,
smiling indulgently as she watched the
little cameo of greeting that passed
between them. Bruce seized the girl,
swung her high in the air, and hugged
her before craning back to look into her
face. Then he kissed her soundly.

Bruce glanced towards Valerie, and

she noted that his face was transformed. Gone was the harsh and defensive manner. His attitude was more natural, his eyes filled with a softer expression. Emotion filled her breast as she watched them.

Mandy was chattering like a magpie. Bruce was listening seriously, nodding his head from time to time. Then, carrying Mandy, he came towards Valerie.

'Valerie, tell Daddy about the pirates on the boat and the smugglers in the cave!' Mandy exclaimed excitedly, her expression alive with pleasure. 'Tell him about the horse, and the pictures you took, and . . . ' She broke off and stared around. 'Where's my teddy?' she cried. 'I've left him in the car! You must see teddy, Daddy.'

'I'll fetch teddy,' Valerie said, catching Bruce's eye as she turned away.

Mandy slid from his arms and hurried to Valerie's side, taking her hand. 'I'll walk with you, Valerie,' she said.

'Did you have a good day, Valerie?' Bruce enquired as she unlocked the car door for Mandy to get the teddy bear.

'We had a marvellous time, didn't we, Valerie?' Mandy demanded, so excited that she didn't give Valerie an opportunity to answer.

'It looks as if I've lost a daughter,' Bruce commented ruefully. 'I don't know what you've done to her, Valerie, but don't stop now. Keep up the good work. She hasn't looked so happy since before . . . ' He broke off, frowning, as if his thoughts were too bitter to contemplate. 'Wait until Doctor Spencer sees her!' he continued. 'You have to see him on Thursday, Mandy.'

'I don't need to see him any more,' Mandy replied chirpily. 'I'm happy now, and that's what Doctor Spencer says I have to concentrate on.'

Valerie relocked the car door, and there was a tingle in her breast as they walked to the main entrance of the hotel. Home and Robert and all the attendant worries were far away from her at this moment.

'Daddy, can Valerie have tea with us?' Mandy demanded.

'Certainly, if she wishes,' he replied without hesitation. He glanced at Valerie, a smile on his lips. 'Would you accept an invitation to have tea with us?' he asked graciously.

'I'd love to stay,' Valerie said instantly. 'In fact, after such a lovely time, I don't really fancy going back to the bungalow and suffering all that solitude.'

'You don't have to,' Bruce said immediately. 'There's a vacant room next to Mandy's that you can use any time you like.' He paused and smiled. 'Free of charge, of course.'

'Will you stay, Valerie?' Mandy demanded pleadingly.

'We'll see,' Valerie said.

She glanced warningly at Bruce. He seemed to think it was a good idea. But she was afraid that if Mandy got used to her being around she'd be very upset when she had to return to London.

'Well, at least you'll have tea with us,'

Bruce said firmly, 'and I won't take no for an answer.'

He held Valerie's gaze as she looked at him, and she could only nod and smile her agreement.

As they entered the lobby, Miss Harper appeared, and she paused at the sight of them. Then she looked more closely at Mandy, who was clutching her teddy bear, a contented smile upon her face.

'What have we here?' Miss Harper demanded, intercepting Mandy and taking the teddy bear. 'A new guest! We don't get many like him these days, I can tell you. What's his name, may I ask?'

She glanced at Valerie before giving her attention to Mandy, and there was approval in her gaze.

'We didn't think of giving him a name,' Valerie said. 'What a shame!'

'I'll call him Adam!' Mandy said breezily.

'Why Adam?' Bruce enquired, puzzled.

'Because I got him from Adamporth!'

Mandy chuckled. 'It was bought for me because I'm a special friend of Valerie's.'

'You're everyone's special friend,' Bruce told her, his eyes holding a gleam which Valerie did not miss. 'I think you and Valerie had better freshen up, don't you? Show Valerie the guest room next to yours, Mandy, and she'll stay if she wants to. But don't be unfair and put undue pressure on her, will you?'

'Of course not,' Mandy said firmly. 'I wouldn't like it if Valerie stayed only because I wanted her to. I'd never ask her to do anything she didn't want to. That's not fair, is it?'

'Now that's what I call a real friend,' Bruce said quietly. 'And it puts me to shame. I don't know what you and Valerie have got going here, but you're making me realise just how badly I've been shirking my duties as a father.' He grinned as Mandy looked up at him, a sudden frown clouding her radiant features. But he merely chuckled at her doubt and went on cheerfully.

'I happen to know that I have no engagements of any kind tomorrow, except one. So bear that in mind, Miss Harper, if anyone calls up wanting my time. To be on the safe side you'd better say I'm away on business until the day after tomorrow.'

'Very well.' Miss Harper inclined her head, then asked, 'What engagement do you have pencilled in for tomorrow?'

'I'm going to take my daughter to Land's End! I was cheated out of her company today, and I intend to make the most of tomorrow. So no appointments under any circumstances, is that clear?'

Miss Harper shrugged. 'You shouldn't say such things in front of Mandy until you're certain you will be free,' she said sharply. 'You've disappointed her too often in the past.'

'That couldn't be helped.' For a moment he looked deadly serious, and Valerie frowned as she watched his changing expression. 'But I'm getting the groundwork behind me now, and there will be more free time after this.'

'I don't mind if you can't take me tomorrow,' Mandy informed him complacently. 'I could go with Valerie.'

'You certainly could,' Valerie said unhesitatingly. 'I have never been to Land's End, and I must see it before I go back to London.'

'I won't go with you, Daddy, unless Valerie can come as well,' Mandy said determinedly.

'You little blackmailer!' Bruce smiled, but his face turned serious as he glanced at Valerie. 'As to that, I'm quite willing to be chauffeur to both of you tomorrow, but Valerie may not want to go with us.'

'As a matter of fact, I intended visiting it tomorrow, and decided that before I met you, Mandy.'

'And would you mind if Daddy came along with us?' Mandy asked seriously.

Both Bruce and Miss Harper chuckled, and Bruce shook his head in mock despair.

'All right,' he said. 'If this is the only

way I can get to go out with my daughter than I'll eat humble pie. I'll beg for the opportunity to go to Land's End, with you both, and promise to be on my best behaviour. I'll even go further. If you'll let me come with you I'll do the driving, and take care of all expenses, no matter what you buy.'

'You don't have to ask me if you want to go with us, Daddy,' Mandy said, trying hard not to giggle. 'It's up to Valerie! She's my special friend, and she may not want anyone else along with us.'

Bruce immediately dropped to his knees, in the middle of the lobby, and clasped his hands together.

'Please!' he said in a loud, pleading voice. 'Please, may I came with you tomorrow?'

Mandy burst into gales of laughter, and Valerie joined in. Miss Harper shook her head and tut-tutted, smiling before turning away to her office.

'Daddy, you look so funny!' Mandy declared, giggling hysterically. She ran to him and threw her arms around his neck. 'I love you, Daddy!'

Suddenly her laughter turned to tears, and she dropped her teddy and wept, her shoulders heaving. Bruce frowned and gathered her up, his concern all too evident.

'What is it, sweetheart?' he demanded. 'Was it something I said?'

'No,' Valerie told him, going to his side and putting a hand on Mandy's shoulder. 'We had this trouble earlier. It's nothing you've said, and it's not something that Mandy can control at the moment. Her eyes seem to have a mind of their own. They just feel like watering at this moment, but they'll stop in a moment, won't they, Mandy?'

'Yes,' the girl said in a muffled voice. 'It's my eyes, Daddy. I'm not crying. I'm not unhappy. My eyes are raining, that's all.'

Bruce looked at Valerie as understanding showed in his face, and he nodded and smiled. 'I understand, Mandy,' he said softly. 'You've found happiness again, and it's difficult to accustom yourself to it. Well, you're not the only one, you know. My eyes have rained a great deal during the past two years, but I have a feeling all that is now behind us, and you'll see a lot of changes in future. Your eyes won't want to rain.'

Valerie nodded and held out her arms for Mandy. Bruce passed her over, and the girl buried her face in Valerie's neck.

'We'll go up to Mandy's room,' Valerie said, 'and we'll both come down to tea as soon as we've freshened up. I expect Mandy is hungry, aren't you, dear?'

'Yes.' The reply was muffled, and Valerie hugged the girl impulsively.

They both disappeared up to Mandy's room and after a short time both of them were nicely freshened up.

They went down to the dining-room and Bruce helped them to their seats.

He sat down opposite, and Valerie couldn't keep her gaze from his clean-cut features. She hadn't liked him at first but now she felt a growing affection for him.

Her musing was interrupted by a smartly-dressed woman who approached their table from behind Bruce's seat.

'There you are, Bruce,' the newcomer declared, pausing at his side.

He looked up, startled by her presence, and then got to his feet.

'Ruth!' he exclaimed, and Valerie fought against the frown that tried to make itself evident between her eyes. 'I didn't expect to see you here! I was going to call you later and arrange a meeting.'

'Yes, you naughty man!' Ruth studied Valerie coolly as she spoke, and Valerie stiffened under the scrutiny. Tension seemed to fill the dining-room, and Valerie was aware that Mandy had tensed and was staring down at the floor.

'How is Mandy today?' Ruth turned her attention to the child, and Mandy grasped Valerie's hand under the table and gripped it tightly. The little girl seemed oddly ill-at-ease.

'I'm very well thank you, Mrs Ordway,' Mandy replied.

Ruth tut-tutted, and a glint appeared in her expressive blue eyes. 'The times I've told you to call me Ruth!' she exclaimed, and fell silent, gazing expectantly at Valerie and obviously awaiting an introduction.

Valerie subconsciously put up her guard. There was something in Ruth's tone and manner which indicated that they could never be friends, and she was startled by her flash of intuition. Ruth's smile seemed artificial, and there was an undercurrent in her manner which did not ring true to Valerie. Then she recalled her father's words over the telephone. He had mentioned Ruth, suspecting that the woman had designs on Bruce, and had hinted that she was a very determined female who would surely get what she wanted. So this was Ruth, Valerie mused as Bruce arose.

'We're about to have tea,' he said. 'Would you care to join us, Ruth? Then later we could go over that little bit of business.'

'You are a terror, you know, Bruce.' Ruth sat down in his seat and he moved to another, his manner urbane.

'I waited in half the afternoon for you to call,' Ruth continued in a slightly over-sweet tone, 'and you left me waiting regardless. Your business isn't so important that you can't leave it for an hour! I really have gone to a great deal of trouble to help you, and this is all the thanks I get for my concern and efforts. What are you playing at?'

'Now, Ruth, you don't want Miss Kenton to get the wrong idea about you, do you?' Bruce demanded, smiling at Valerie.

'And who is Miss Kenton?' Ruth demanded, looking narrowly at Valerie as if becoming aware of her presence for the very first time.

'She's my special friend,' Mandy piped up. 'It's Valerie. She saved me on

76

the cliff. If she hadn't found me I might have fallen like my mummy did.'

Bruce tightened his lips at the reminder of their personal tragedy, and Valerie frowned. But Ruth merely smiled, as if Mandy had said something amusing. She was tall and willowy, strikingly beautiful, and probably in her late 20s. There was a large diamond ring on the engagement finger of her left hand which Valerie couldn't help wondering about.

'This is Valerie Kenton,' Bruce introduced. 'Valerie, meet Ruth Ordway.'

Valerie leaned forward, prepared to shake hands, but Ruth merely stared at her without moving a muscle, and suddenly the woman's eyes were the coldest Valerie had ever seen.

As the meal progressed it became obvious that Ruth intended monopolising Bruce's attention, but he was more than a match for her, and kept bringing Valerie into the conversation with cleverly-phrased questions that needed direct answers. He was completely at ease, and smiled encouragingly every time his glance met Valerie's.

'Where are you from, Valerie?' he asked, when it seemed that Ruth's boldness would force him into an agreement he seemed loath to accept.

'London,' Valerie replied quietly, and he chuckled.

'Are you planning to stay here long?' Ruth demanded. 'I think you will find life dull after the bright lights.'

'On the contrary,' Valerie replied. 'I find Cornwall quite charming.' She glanced at Mandy, who seemed to have no interest in their conversation. The girl was engrossed with her tea, but smiled when she met Valerie's gaze. 'Mind you, I've had some very pleasant company since I arrived,' Valerie added, and was rewarded with a chuckle from Mandy.

'Can we go out after tea, Valerie?' the girl demanded. 'It's been such a lovely day that I don't want it to end.'

'We'll see when the time comes,' Valerie replied, and Ruth stared intently, obviously trying to work out the situation.

'When do you go back to London, may I ask?' Ruth demanded.

Valerie smiled disarmingly and shrugged.

'I really have no idea. I'm on an open-ended holiday. It doesn't finish on any specific date. If I enjoy myself I'll stay on until I have had enough.'

'You would have been better suited in Paris, or one of the other big cities,' Ruth declared.

Valerie smiled. 'You're judging me by my appearance,' she observed.

Bruce put down his knife and fork and pushed aside his almost finished meal. He smiled ruefully as he looked at Valerie.

'Would you excuse me?' he said quietly. 'I've just remembered that I had to make a phone call the minute I reached the hotel, but meeting Mandy out in the car park knocked it completely out of my head. I also have some office work to sort out before I can satisfy myself that I can take tomorrow off with a clear conscience.'

'You're having a day off tomorrow?' Ruth demanded, pushing aside her plate and rising as Bruce stood up. 'Well it's about time. I've been begging you for months to take me to the Scillies.'

'I'm sorry but tomorrow has already been settled,' he replied. 'I'm taking Mandy and Valerie to Land's End for the day.' He glanced at Mandy. 'That's if my daughter still wants to go,' he added.

'Yes please,' Mandy said loudly. 'And with Valerie coming with us it will be as good as when we used to go out for the day with Mummy.'

'I plan to make it as good as I possibly can,' Bruce replied.

He turned away, and Ruth stared intently at Valerie before hurrying after him. Valerie sat for a moment, dismayed by Ruth's manner. The woman had an overpowering personality.

Mandy picked up her glass of milk and drank deeply before remarking upon Ruth.

'I don't like her,' she said with the candour of innocence, 'because she doesn't like me. My mummy didn't like her either. I don't know why she always comes to the hotel, or why she has to see Daddy so much about business.'

There were questions Valerie would like to have asked but she refrained from asking them. It was really none of her business if Ruth was trying to get Bruce to marry her. But she was dismayed at the thought of Mandy's future with Ruth as her stepmother . . .

5

Valerie didn't stay the night at the hotel. She remained until Mandy went to bed. Valerie left the room with the girl's goodnight and blessings echoing in her ears, and sighed deeply as she went down to the lobby.

Miss Harper was sitting at her desk, drinking coffee. She looked utterly weary, but got to her feet when Valerie appeared.

'Please don't get up,' Valerie begged. 'I just want to tell you that Mandy's in bed and probably asleep by now. I'm going home, and I've arranged that Mandy and her father will pick me up at my bungalow around nine-thirty in the morning. Would you pass that on to Mr Stirling in case Mandy gets it muddled?'

'I think you'd better pass on the message in person, Valerie,' Miss

Harper responded. 'Mr Stirling is in the bar waiting for you. He wants to thank you for the way you've taken Mandy under your wing.'

She went to the bar and peered in. Bruce was talking to the barman, and he must have been watching for her because he straightened immediately and came to her, a welcoming smile on his handsome face.

'Hello,' he greeted. 'Has Mandy finally retired? You must have found her quite exhausting today!'

'Not really.' Valerie shook her head. 'Poor girl! She's got a lot of forgetting to do. But she was very good company!'

'You've certainly set her feet on the right path, and I don't know how to begin thanking you.' He sighed and shook his head. 'If you're not too tired we could have a chat. Would you like a drink?'

'Thank you. A white wine, please.' Valerie accompanied him to a vacant table near the bar and sat down while he went to get the drinks.

Bruce returned and placed a drink before her, smiling as their gazes met. Then he sat down opposite and sipped from a tall glass. Valerie tensed unaccountably, and drew a deep breath as she picked up her glass.

'Is that OK for you?' he enquired, his dark eyes gleaming.

Valerie felt suddenly warm. 'It's fine, thanks,' she said with a catch in her voice, and wondered why she was getting excited. But she knew why! Her emotions had been stirred by Mandy! Tenderness filled her as she pictured the girl's face. And her father had told Miss Harper he wouldn't mind if she stayed here at least a month!

'I really appreciate what you've done for Mandy in the last two days,' Bruce said slowly. 'I've been at my wits' end for months, trying to get her back to normal. She's had two governesses since Christmas, and neither could make any headway with her. It wasn't that she was ill-behaved or unruly! She was just so withdrawn that they failed to make contact with her. Then you turned up and a miracle occurred! Mandy is almost back to normal!' He shook his head and sighed deeply. 'I only hope it lasts!'

'If you give her some of your time and make her feel wanted and loved I'm sure she'll maintain the progress she's made.' Valerie sipped her drink and studied him over the rim of the glass. He seemed in need of love and attention himself! The thought formed in her mind, and she set down her glass, stifling a sigh.

'Business will take a back seat where Mandy is concerned.' He spoke firmly, and she guessed that he meant what he said. 'Is it all right for us to go to Land's End tomorrow? I feel guilty about taking up your time.'

'Don't give it a second thought. While I'm here I'll do anything I can to help Mandy. I'm not really on holiday. I came here to get away from a situation back home which should settle itself while I'm away.' She gazed at him as if expecting to be challenged, but he merely nodded.

'That's how I figured it,' he said. 'So may I ask a favour of you? I have engaged another governess for Mandy, someone who has nursing qualifications and understands her kind of problem. But she's unable to take up her appointment for another two weeks, and you're working such wonders with Mandy that I have to ask if you would care to consider a temporary job as companion to her. I'd see that you have plenty of free time.' He paused and awaited her reaction.

'If you think my company would help Mandy then I'll see what I can do.'

'Thank you.' He nodded. 'I'll be forever in your debt. Mandy is all I have in the world now, and I must ensure her happiness. Now what about remuneration? What would you consider a fair salary for two weeks? Shall I open negotiations with a figure of five hundred pounds?'

'Five hundred pounds!' Valerie stared

at him in amazement. 'For two weeks? My goodness! I don't want a penny! I'll take care of Mandy solely for the pleasure of her company.'

'But I couldn't possibly accept those terms!' He shook his head emphatically. 'You must be paid!'

'Technically, I'm not free to take other employment,' she retorted, smiling. 'So I refuse to consider it as a job. It will have to be on my terms or not at all! I don't want payment.'

He shrugged helplessly, considered for a moment, and then nodded. 'All right, I know when I've met my match! It will be on your terms, but I insist that you move into the hotel for the rest of your stay in Cornwall, for which, of course, you won't get a bill.'

Valerie caught her breath. Suddenly, feeling close to tears, she became aware of the reason why Mandy had managed to touch her heart. The girl had lost her mother two years ago, and Valerie's mother had died when Valerie was quite young. That was the bond between them!

'Fine,' she agreed. 'I'll stay at the bungalow tonight, and when we come back from Land's End tomorrow I'll bring my clothes here.'

'Thank you.' He reached across the table and took hold of her hand before she realised what he was doing. 'I don't know how I'm ever going to be able to thank you adequately,' he remarked, releasing her hand and leaning back in his seat. 'I'm quite looking forward to tomorrow, you know. I haven't had a day off for months. I'm planning a large-scale pleasure complex here, and there's been so much to do. But I think I've broken the back of it now, and hereafter it should be much easier for all concerned.'

'Mandy will benefit from seeing you more often,' Valerie suggested. She finished her drink. 'If I don't leave now I shall be tired in the morning! It's been quite an eventful day, and tomorrow promises to be the same.'

'You have your car outside,' he

mused. 'If you don't mind, I'll see you to your bungalow. It's dark now, and you shouldn't go home alone. Rajah hasn't had any exercise today so I have to take him for a walk anyway.'

'Thank you.' She nodded and stood up.

'I'll fetch Rajah. Come and wait in the lobby.' He took their glasses to the bar and they walked into the lobby together.

Valerie waited by the reception desk while Bruce fetched Rajah. When he returned with the dog at his heels, Rajah made a dive for her. She patted him and he licked her effusively.

'I've never seen that dog take to anyone as he has to you,' Bruce remarked. 'I have to keep him locked up when Ruth is around. He always looks as if he'd like to bite her.'

'Perhaps she doesn't like dogs,' Valerie countered, 'and Rajah would sense that.'

'There's a lot that Ruth doesn't like,' he mused, and led the way to the door.

Valerie followed him outside.

Valerie drove to the bungalow with Bruce beside her and Rajah in the back seat. She tried to analyse her feelings in the silence that ensued. Two days ago she'd been unaware of the existence of Bruce or Mandy, and now their paths had crossed. She frowned as she considered the moment when she would have to return to London. Her father had said something about not getting involved with Mandy, and now she knew what he meant, for Mandy could be hurt when the time of parting came.

They alighted at the bungalow, and Bruce insisted on going in first to check for intruders.

'I'm not being unduly cautious,' he remarked. 'We have quite a spate of break-ins around this time of the year, although if the place is seen to be occupied then usually it's left alone.' He paused and glanced around. 'If you like I'll leave Rajah here with you tonight. He'd certainly scare off any prowler.'

'Thank you, that's thoughtful of you, but I'm not afraid to be on my own.'

'Fine. Then I'll see you in the morning around nine-thirty.' He smiled. 'Sleep well. Goodnight. Come along, Rajah.'

'Goodnight,' she replied.

Valerie locked the door and leaned against it, her mind in a whirl. She heard Rajah bark several times, the sound getting fainter as master and dog walked back along the cliffs, and wished that she was out there with them! The desire came from nowhere, and she tried to control her emotions. What was happening to her? Was this change due to leaving home, or were Mandy and her father having this strange effect upon her?

She showered and then went to bed, tossing and turning for a period.

Eventually she fell asleep only to be woken by sunlight streaming into her window. She lay, for a while, luxuriating in the cosy warmth of the bed. Then she glanced at her watch and realised it was time to move or she wouldn't be ready by nine-thirty.

While getting ready, she considered Mandy and Bruce. She was happy to be taking charge of the girl for the next two weeks. That side of it was clear-cut and obvious. But, when her thoughts turned to Bruce, she experienced a strange restlessness.

She continued trying to analyse her feelings during breakfast. But she couldn't clarify her emotions towards Bruce! Since they were practically strangers she should have no feelings for him at all! But an image of his face was imprinted upon the screen of her mind, and she experienced an occasional tug of pure emotion. She caught herself glancing at her wrist watch too frequently, and realised that she was instinctively listening for the approach of Bruce's car.

When the telephone rang she leaped to her feet to answer. Bruce spoke her name, and the sound of his voice sent an undefinable thrill through her.

'Valerie, I can't make the trip today,'

he said harshly. 'Something's come up that I can't really postpone, and I feel terrible about Mandy. I haven't told her yet, and she's out there in the lobby waiting to come and pick you up. What can I do? This will break her heart!'

'Don't tell her anything at the moment,' Valerie said instinctively. 'I'm ready at this end, and I'll come to the hotel right away. It might be better if we say that I'm the one who can't make it today, and if I've judged her right she'll probably ask you to postpone the outing until I can go along. That would be better than having her feel that you've let her down again.'

'That's quick thinking, and I appreciate it,' he said instantly. 'But what excuse can you give for calling it off?'

'Tell her I've just called and complained of not feeling well. Will your business take all day?'

'I have to go into Plymouth, and that's thirty miles from here. It's finance, Valerie, and I can't postpone it. My partner is in the area unexpectedly, and I must meet with him.'

'That's all right. I'm sure you'd make it if you could. The main consideration is Mandy. I don't mind telling a white lie if it will save her from further unhappiness. I'll take her out somewhere today and get her mind off it. Then you must make further arrangements to take her out for the day as soon as possible. You must do that to keep her happy.'

'Thank you! I'll tell Mandy that you've called, and leave the rest until you arrive. Don't be long, will you?'

'I'm on my way,' Valerie replied, and hung up.

She was conscious of disappointment herself as she drove to the hotel. But her subconscious mind was working at the situation, and when she alighted from the car and spotted Mandy coming to greet her she steeled herself for what could only prove to be an ordeal.

'Valerie! Daddy said you telephoned! What's wrong? Why can't you go to

Land's End today? Are you ill? I've been so looking forward to going! I was awake half the night thinking about it!'

'I'm sorry, Mandy. I have such a bad headache that I couldn't possibly travel in a car. But you and Daddy could go alone, unless you'd rather call it off until I'm feeling better.'

'Poor Valerie! Does your head hurt much?' Mandy grasped Valerie's hand and began to lead her into the hotel. 'We won't go today! Daddy will be disappointed, but if you don't feel well we can make it another day!'

Bruce appeared in the doorway as they reached the top step, his face expressionless. Mandy clutched Valerie's arm even tighter as she passed on the bad news.

'Daddy, poor Valerie isn't feeling well so we can't go to Land's End! I'll stay here and look after her. You could take us out another day, couldn't you?'

'Quite easily,' he replied, coming to Valerie's side and grasping her arm. 'I must say you do look pale. Perhaps

Mandy was too much for you yesterday!' He winked, and Valerie compressed her lips. 'But not to worry,' he continued. 'We can certainly go out another day. It's a great pity though! I was looking forward to Land's End today.'

'Valerie can lie down in my room,' Mandy said solicitously.

'It's all right,' Valerie said instantly. 'What I really need is some fresh air. A nice long walk along the cliffs will do me good. Then if I feel better later we could think of something else to do.' She looked at Bruce.

'I'm thinking about the outing to Land's End,' he said. 'If I leave now I can get tomorrow's work done today, and then we can get away when you feel better.'

'Can you really do that, Daddy?' Mandy asked doubtfully.

'I'll try, sweetheart!' He turned his attention to Valerie. 'Are you sure you'll be all right if I leave you in Mandy's hands?'

'Of course she'll be all right with me,'

Mandy said indignantly. 'I'll take her for a walk. She'll get plenty of fresh air. You'd better go and start on tomorrow's work, Daddy, or we won't be able to go out when Valerie is better. We'll all go to Land's End together.'

Bruce smiled. He threw a grateful look at Valerie, who grimaced at him, then he sighed heavily and departed. Mandy shook Valerie's arm.

'Come on,' she said. 'Let's go for a walk. Did you have some breakfast? Missing that could give you a headache.'

Valerie smiled ruefully as she allowed Mandy to lead her towards the cliffs. She saw Bruce get into his car and drive off. When she looked at Mandy there was nothing but concern showing in the girl's face, and she realised that their little subterfuge had really spared the girl the keen disappointment that Valerie herself was feeling . . .

The day passed, and Mandy occupied herself with fussing over Valerie. They walked along the cliffs, and, on the way back to the hotel, Valerie explained the arrangement she had made with Bruce. Mandy stared at her with pleasure showing in her dark eyes.

'Two whole weeks!' she exclaimed, clapping her hands. 'That's super! I know about Miss Cannell coming and I hope she'll be better than the other two companions I had! But you've made me feel much better, Valerie.' She paused and considered. 'I wish you could be my companion. We'd have so much fun!'

'Now I'm feeling better why don't we go back to the hotel for my car and then collect my clothes from the bungalow?' Valerie suggested. 'I'm to have the room next to yours for the next two weeks!'

Mandy was all in favour of the idea, and they spent the rest of the day settling Valerie into the hotel. Towards evening, Valerie began to watch for Bruce's return, but by the time Mandy was ready for bed he hadn't put in an appearance.

'Daddy is usually late,' Mandy said as she snuggled down the bed. 'But never mind. We've still got Land's End to look forward to. I'm glad we didn't go today because the fun would be over now, and we've still got it to look forward to. We'll have a great day.'

Valerie was thoughtful as she went down to the lobby to telephone her father. She was missing Bruce! The knowledge hit her, but she was no longer surprised by the fact. Bruce was a very nice man and she liked him!

But they did not get to Land's End at all during that week. Bruce had too much to do, and his daily apology became routine as the days passed. However, Mandy was quite fatalistic, although she kept close to Valerie's side, and Valerie was the only one to suffer the disappointments of Bruce's repeated postponement of the outing.

Then, more than a week after the initial arrangement, they set out for Land's End. Bruce had finally managed to get a free day. As they got into his car, Valerie couldn't help thinking over the week that had ensued since she moved into the hotel. The odd occasions when she saw Bruce had served only to intensify her emotions.

Now she accepted, with a degree of fatalism, that she was falling in love with him, despite the fact that Ruth Ordway was well and truly ensconced in his life. Her eyes darkened as she recalled the instances she had seen Ruth with Bruce. The woman always made it obvious that she had designs on him.

'Valerie!' Mandy's face was shining, her hair immaculately groomed. 'Are you feeling all right today?'

'Very much so.' Valerie clasped the girl's hand. 'We're going to enjoy today, don't you think?'

'I know we shall,' the girl replied, 'and I'm glad we didn't go to Land's End last week.'

'It's going to be a very nice day,' Bruce remarked as they drove away from the hotel. 'Mandy must have said her prayers last night.' He chuckled. 'I know I did. So here's to us having a great time.'

He was dressed casually in brown trousers and a beige shirt. A tweed sports-jacket lay on the back seat. Valerie thought how attractive he looked and was acutely aware of his proximity as they drove through St Austell and took the road to Truro.

There was much to see in the countryside, and Bruce called out the sights as they appeared. Just before reaching Penzance they spotted St Michael's Mount, and Mandy clapped her hands in excitement.

'Can we see that another day, Daddy?' she demanded excitedly. 'You promised last week that you'd take me out several times.'

'So I did,' he retorted, smiling at Valerie. 'We'll have to see what we can do, shan't we?'

Valerie tried to control the tingling sensation that enveloped her. From time to time she stole glances at Bruce's profile, and admiration filled her. She found him increasingly attractive.

After a pleasant drive they turned into the large car park at Land's End. Despite the early season there were quite a lot of visitors. Valerie turned slowly to survey the scene while Bruce locked the car. Tall cliffs confronted the sea, where a lighthouse was visible a long way out. The sea was calm, and sunlight dappled the water.

Bruce came to stand at Valerie's side, his arm touching her shoulder. She almost recoiled, for the contact was like receiving an electric shock. But Mandy clutched at her hand and the moment passed. She breathed deeply, causing Bruce to glance at her with narrowed eyes.

'If you're not used to this scenery it is apt to take your breath away,' he observed.

'It certainly does,' she responded, relieved to find an excuse.

There were a number of exhibitions to see; a display featuring Man and the

Sea, and a video theatre with running commentary. Then they passed through rooms containing the history of Air-Sea Rescue and the Lifeboat Service. Bruce was engrossed by the subject, and even Mandy was interested when Bruce explained some of the points of interest.

'Ruth's husband was a lifeboatman, wasn't he, Daddy?' Mandy asked, and Valerie glanced at Bruce as he replied.

'Yes. Brian was a very brave man.' A harsh note stiffened Bruce's voice and Valerie frowned. 'He was a close friend,' Bruce went on. 'He died in a local lifeboat tragedy some time ago.'

'They're all brave men,' Valerie responded.

After the exhibitions it was time for Cornish ice-cream, and they sat at a wooden table to enjoy it. Then they went into the craft workshops at State House. Valerie saw a Cornish pisky, worked in glass, and, the minute she admired it, Bruce bought it, smiling when she demurred.

'Mandy's gift for you,' he informed her.

Valerie nodded and graciously accepted the little, white cardboard box.

'I told Daddy he would have to buy the very first thing you said you liked,' Mandy asserted.

Valerie smiled as she thanked the girl, and Bruce smiled. They went on to have their photograph taken under the famous Land's End signpost, and Bruce bought three copies, which he put into his pocket.

'I'll keep them safe until later, Valerie,' he said. 'You'll need a snap to remind you what Mandy looks like when you go back to London.'

Valerie nodded, but the knowledge that all this would have to come to an end filled her with gloom. She saw a shadow cross Mandy's face, and knew the child was thinking the same. She patted the girl's shoulder, and Mandy looked up at her.

'Enjoying yourself?' Valerie asked.

Mandy nodded, but her eyes showed

doubt, and Valerie could only guess at what was passing through her mind.

They spent another hour at Land's End, and Valerie enjoyed a Cornish pasty in the restaurant. Then they browsed through the souvenir shops, where Valerie bought Mandy several small souvenirs and helped the girl choose something for Bruce. Afterwards, it was time to leave, and they made their reluctant way back to the car.

6

Valerie was relaxed and comfortable as Bruce drove homewards, and she felt a great sense of euphoria that she'd never experienced before. Whenever she glanced at him she felt the power of his attraction, and her face burned unnaturally as emotive thoughts emerged from the recesses of her mind. Several times she checked that Mandy was all right, and Bruce chuckled when he noticed her action.

'You're just like a mother hen with a day-old chick!' he observed. 'I've been watching you all morning, Valerie, and, although you don't fuss, you won't let the wind blow on Mandy.'

Valerie smiled. 'That poor child needs looking after. She's lacking a great deal.'

'You make it sound as if I've been neglecting her!' He glanced at her, strong hands steady on the steering-wheel. But there was a friendly note in his tone, and she realised how changed he seemed compared with the rather gruff man she'd encountered on their initial meeting.

'Taking today off and relaxing with Mandy is doing you a lot of good, too,' she said, and he chuckled.

'I have enjoyed myself,' he admitted, 'but I can't afford to relax now. What I'm doing is safeguarding Mandy's future. I'm aware that I drive myself very hard, but that's how it's been since my wife died.'

'It must have been dreadful for you!'

Valerie was greatly sympathetic, and he glanced at her, a slight frown upon his handsome features.

'You sound as if you might know something about that sort of thing,' he mused. 'I know your father is still alive. Have you lost your mother?'

'Yes, when I was just a girl. So I know how Mandy's been feeling, and that's why I'm determined to help her.'

'Well, your approach is perfect,' he observed. 'I didn't think it was possible, the speed with which she reacted to you. Thank goodness you came along, Valerie.'

She smiled, liking the sound of her name upon his lips. When she risked a glance at him it was to find that he was watching her out of a corner of his eye and he smiled as their glances met.

'You know, I could quite easily accept that you are supernatural. You appeared from nowhere at a time when people don't usually take a holiday, and you charmed my dog and captured the imagination of my daughter. What are you, Valerie? A good fairy sent to cure some of the apparent ills that seem to have befallen us?'

'Stranger things have happened,' she countered. 'These days, nothing is impossible.'

'Well, I think you're out of this world! There aren't many women who would make such an effort to help Mandy.' He sighed heavily. 'I know some who have tried to use her as a means of getting to me!' He shrugged. 'But that's something else. You're completely selfless! And you're not having a very good holiday.' He shook his head slowly. 'Aren't you interested in the bright lights? What made you bury yourself in Cornwall?'

'I thought I explained! I needed to get away from a situation that had developed at home.'

'Did you fight with your father?'

'No.' She shook her head. 'It was nothing like that. A boyfriend proposed and I turned him down. I didn't like hurting him, but I didn't see any future for us together.'

'And that's why you left home?' He was frowning when she glanced at him. 'That's no reason to run away.'

'I didn't run away! I knew Robert would pester me to go back to him so I took the easy way out. He doesn't know where I am, and while I'm here he can't get at me.'

'He doesn't know where you are?'

'That's right. And Dad won't tell him.'

'So you're not the marrying kind!' He grimaced. 'That's odd. I could have sworn you'd make a perfect wife.'

'Robert is obviously the wrong man for me.' She tried to dispel the tension which suddenly filled her. 'I was aware of it for quite some time before he proposed, but I didn't think he was that serious about me.'

'It's fortunate that you discovered your true feelings before it was too late.' His expression was profound. 'Marriage is a very serious business. Too many people treat it too lightly these days.'

She nodded, her thoughts returning to her home. She pictured Robert and suppressed a sigh. Her main concern was that she was unable to fall in love sufficiently enough to go through the whole process of selection and marriage. She glanced at Bruce and wondered what it would be like to be loved by such a man. She sensed she'd become infatuated, but was wise enough to realise that perhaps sympathy was at the root of it and not some deeper emotion. Her feelings were all rather confusing.

Mandy awoke a little later and leaned over the back of Valerie's seat. Her face was flushed and her eyes filled with sleep. She smiled and laid her head against Valerie's shoulder.

'Had a good sleep?' Valerie enquired, and Mandy nodded. 'That's great! It's done you good.'

'Are we going home?' Mandy glanced around. 'I thought we were out for the day, Daddy!'

'It's early yet,' Bruce acknowledged with a chuckle. 'And we really should make the most of our free time. So any suggestions concerning our next destination will be thankfully received.'

'It's up to you, Mandy,' Valerie prompted. 'I'm a stranger here and I have no idea where the sights are.'

'You choose somewhere, Daddy,' Mandy said. 'I don't mind where it is so long as we don't go back to the hotel yet.'

'It's only three o'clock,' Bruce remarked. 'Shall we go into Truro and look around? The shops won't close until five-thrity, and there are one or two things I'd like to buy you, Mandy.'

'Buy me?' Mandy's voice became edged with excitement.

'Clothes and the like!' Bruce laughed. 'And I think we ought to take advantage of Valerie's dress sense to fit you out with a new wardrobe. Summer will soon be upon us and we should be prepared for it.'

Mandy clapped her hands and gave vent to an excited cry. Valerie smiled. To her mind, Mandy had made immeasurable progress. She was now beyond the danger of relapse and it hadn't taken much to pull the girl round! Her behaviour today was that of any other little girl.

They stopped in Truro and began a round of the shops. Mandy enjoyed trying on new clothes. The sound of her excited chatter and laughter was as happy as any normal youngster's should be.

Valerie was keenly aware that there was only another week in which to guide the girl, and she hoped she'd see Bruce every day. She studied his face when he wasn't looking, her mind constantly adding to the image it was building up.

When they were helping Mandy out of a summer dress their hands touched, and Valerie recoiled as if she'd been burned. Bruce noticed her reaction and frowned. But he made no comment. Valerie felt awkward and was further discomfited when she felt her cheeks burning. Mandy noticed her nervousness and was immediately worried.

'You haven't got another headache, have you?' she asked with concern. 'We'll go home if you like.'

'It's all right.' Valerie smiled. 'I'm finding it a bit airless in here, that's all.'

'Are you sure you're all right?' Bruce demanded. 'This shopping spree isn't important. We could come back another time.' He paused, awaiting her decision, a strong hand grasping her elbow.

She fought against the urge to lean against him. What's happening to me, she thought. Am I sickening for something? Then Bruce put an arm around her, and strength seemed to emanate from him. She leaned against him, suddenly dizzy.

'I think we'd better postpone the rest of our shopping and take Valerie home,' Bruce decided. 'Perhaps we've done too much today. And it's my fault. I kept harping on about the fact that I don't have much time to spare, and we hurried around when we do have all the time in the world.'

'I'm all right, really,' Valerie said firmly. 'Let's get on with the shopping.'

'No.' Bruce shook his head. 'What we could do is have a cup of tea, and I know the very place. Come along, Mandy. You must look after Valerie better than this. We'll finish your shopping another day.'

They left the shop, with Mandy holding Valerie's hand, and Bruce carrying the purchases already made. Valerie breathed deeply when they reached the open air, and Bruce grasped her elbow. She thrilled to his touch as they walked along the crowded pavement to a little restaurant.

Valerie made an effort to regain her poise. She'd never experienced anything like this before! She wasn't ill! It had been purely emotional, and she fancied that it was nothing more than a nervous reaction.

A cup of tea worked wonders for her, and she smiled reassuringly when she saw that Mandy was worried.

'I'm fine now,' she insisted. 'Don't worry about me. Come on, let's get on with the shopping. We haven't finished yet.'

Bruce rose and came around the table to grasp Valerie's arm. But at that moment Ruth Ordway appeared, smiling, and her over-sweet tone echoed across the restaurant.

'Bruce, I've rung the hotel half a dozen times since lunch to discover if you'd returned. Where on earth have you been? It's not like you to stop working in the middle of the day. And when I rang your office they insisted that you wouldn't be putting in an appearance until tomorrow!'

'That's right.' He smiled. 'I'm unobtainable today, whatever the reason. I'm entertaining a very important young woman and her companion.'

Valerie didn't miss the furious glance that Ruth bestowed upon her, and realised she was being blamed for this particular situation. But Ruth merely smiled and shook her head, while Valerie couldn't take her eyes off the large, diamond ring on the woman's engagement finger. She wondered who'd put it there, and it slowly dawned on her it might possibly have been Bruce.

'You'll be taking Mandy back to the hotel shortly, won't you?' Ruth demanded. 'And you can't be taking her out all evening as well! Why, she looks half-asleep and ready for bed, this minute! You can spare me a little time later, surely!'

Bruce nodded, and Valerie felt some of the pleasure drain out of her.

'Very well,' Bruce said. 'I'll come over to your place about nine. Will that do?'

'It will be better than nothing, I suppose, so it will have to do.' Ruth spoke grudgingly. She turned away, but not before throwing a harsh glance at Valerie. 'Try to be early,' she called over her shoulder.

Their sense of fun seemed to desert them after Ruth had departed, and Valerie could see a change of mood in Bruce. She found it difficult to contain her own emotions, and was frowning as they left the restaurant.

'I think we'd better call it a day now,' Bruce remarked, leading them back to the car.

Mandy said nothing, but it was evident that she was upset by Ruth's appearance. There was silence in the car until they'd left Truro and were motoring back to the hotel. Then Bruce spoke curtly.

'You're rather quiet, Mandy,' he observed. 'Are you tired?'

'Yes, Daddy.' The girl laid her head against Valerie's shoulder.

Silence ensued again, and then Mandy asked, 'What will happen when Miss Cannell comes next week, Daddy? Will Valerie have to go back to London?'

A pang wrenched at Valerie's heart and she compressed her lips.

'It's up to Valerie when she leaves. She can stay at the hotel as long as she wishes after Miss Cannell's arrival.'

'Shall we see you again after you leave, Valerie?' Mandy persisted. 'I'll miss you! Why can't you stay in Cornwall? You don't have to go back to London, do you?'

'You could always write to me,' Valerie said, aware of a nagging pain in her breast as she considered that the future would be bleak without Mandy and Bruce in it. She tried to fight off the depression which strove to overwhelm her, and realised that Mandy needed to be protected from the trauma of parting.

As they went on, Mandy seemed to withdraw into a shell, and they reached the hotel with hardly another word being spoken. As they drew into the car park, Bruce glanced at Valerie.

'Thank you for being such a good sport,' he said, seemingly recovered from their meeting with Ruth. 'Your company made all the difference today. I really don't know what we would have done without you.'

'Can't you make Valerie stay with us, Daddy?' Mandy demanded. 'I have such good fun with her.'

'Valerie's home's in London,' Bruce said quietly, 'and she'll have to return there when her holiday is over. She's already stayed longer than she originally planned, and that was to help us out. So, we mustn't repay her kindness by unsettling her with selfish demands that she can't possibly meet. That would be most unfair.'

Valerie took Mandy's arm as they alighted from the car, able to tell by the girl's expression that she was miserable. But she realised they'd have to be cruel to be kind. Mandy was well on the way to recovering from the shock of her mother's death, but now she had to be weaned away from Valerie herself.

'Don't worry, Mandy,' she said softly as they waited for Bruce to lock the car and join them. 'We've still got a week together.'

'And you may change your mind about leaving,' Mandy said quickly, her smile returning.

Valerie said no more on the subject, and they entered the dining-room for tea. Afterwards, Bruce excused himself and Valerie escorted Mandy up to their rooms. Mandy was quiet. Valerie could see that the child was upset but she made no comment. Perhaps she would recover more easily if no further mention was made of the near future.

After Mandy had gone to bed, Valerie went into her own room and sat down at the telephone, to call her father. Miss Harper had told her he'd phoned while she was out. When she heard his voice her spirits rose, and she greeted him warmly.

'Val!' he exclaimed. 'How are you getting on? Did you have a nice time today? I phoned earlier and Miss Harper told me you were going out with Mandy and her father.'

'We had a lovely time, Dad.'

'They're all very pleased at the way the child has taken to you,' Jim Kenton continued. 'But have you thought of the problems that could arise when you decide to come home? Or are you remaining in Cornwall indefinitely? That's a decision only you can make.'

'That thought never crossed my mind, Dad,' she replied. 'What are you reading into this situation? All I'm trying to do is help Mandy get over her grief, and I seem to be making a pretty good job of it.'

'Of course, love! You go ahead and enjoy yourself. Heaven knows you deserve a break. Did Miss Harper tell you that I said you were to stay down there for a full month at least?'

'So it's at least a month now, is it?' Valerie sighed. 'I couldn't possibly stay away from the garage that long. How on earth are you managing without me? Or have you discovered that you can do without me?'

'That's not the case and you know it,' he retorted. 'Hey, you sound as if you're under stress. Has anything happened to upset you?'

'No, of course not.'

'You'd tell me if you did have a problem, wouldn't you, Val?'

'You'd be the first to know,' she replied lightly. Then her tone became more serious. 'I think a problem is beginning to rear its head,' she mused and explained about Mandy. 'So you see,' she ended, 'when I do leave here that child is going to be hurt again.' She sighed heavily. 'What do I do, Dad? Any ideas on how the situation can be resolved?'

'From what I've heard it would be perfect all round if you fell in love with Bruce Stirling, married him and became a mother to the girl.'

'I'm being serious, Dad,' she rebuked.

'And so am I,' he retorted.

'Well, that's not much of a solution.' Valerie's eyes narrowed as she tried to think of a way out. 'It's not practical. Things don't work out like that in real life.'

'What do you think of Bruce?' Jim asked.

'He's a nice man with a lot of problems on his mind. But he's getting over the death of his wife, and there's a woman here who seems determined to marry him.'

'Ruth Ordway.' He chuckled. 'Yes. I've met her. It will be the worst day's work Bruce ever does if he marries her!'

Valerie secretly agreed, and changed the subject. 'What's the situation like at home now?' she demanded.

'Robert, do you mean? I don't see so much of him now. The first week you were away was tough all round. He never let a day go by without pestering me for your whereabouts. But I saw him a couple of days ago and he seemed to have calmed down. But you'd better give it another two weeks at least, Val. I think that would be best.'

'I must admit I'm enjoying the break,' she responded. 'It'd be nice if you could come down for a week-end, you know. Why don't you think about it?'

'I have, and I don't think I could manage right now. I like you to be around here while I'm away.'

'All right.' She prepared to hang up. 'I'll call you again tomorrow evening, Dad. Don't work too hard!'

He chuckled. 'And you enjoy yourself, Val. Give my regards to Miss Harper. I shall probably take a holiday at the bungalow later this year. Goodbye now. And look after yourself.'

'Goodbye, Dad.' Valerie hung up and sat back with a sigh. She stared at the telephone as she mulled over the situation.

What could she do about Mandy? Had it been wrong to befriend the girl? But surely it was better to have brought Mandy out of her grief. Although she was tired, Valerie felt an urge to see Bruce, but she was aware that he'd agreed to see Ruth so there'd be no point in going down to the bar. She decided to go to bed, and when she retired, she lay sleepless, her mind roving over the events of the day.

Eventually she slept, and extremely well, considering. When she awoke in the morning she felt more optimistic about the future. At least, she told herself, she'd cleared up the situation between Robert and herself. But now there was Bruce, and she couldn't believe that she'd actually become infatuated with him. How had it happened? What kind of magic had been woven in her mind?

She arose and prepared to face the new day, hoping that by the end of it a solution would have presented itself. But, although she took Mandy out and they had fun, she didn't see Bruce and was no nearer a solution by the time they called it a day.

The week passed quickly, each day coming and going like a dream. As the week-end approached, Valerie began to feel trapped and was unable to think clearly. What would happen when Miss Cannell took up her duties on Monday? Would it be an appropriate time to bow out of Mandy's life and say goodbye to Bruce?

Miss Cannell was due to arrive at the hotel on Sunday, and on Saturday morning Bruce informed them that he'd the day off and was at their service. Valerie was happy to enjoy his company, and they went for a long drive, seeing the sights and visiting noted pleasure spots. Valerie was torn between two powerful emotions. She was keenly aware that her time in

Cornwall was drawing to a close, and that she was in love with Bruce!

Even the sound of Bruce's voice thrilled her, and she found it difficult to remain passive in his company. Whenever he stood beside her she experienced a thrill, and was downcast because he seemed impervious to her presence. He chatted with her as if they were friends of long standing, but he never gave the slightest indication that he was aware of her as a woman.

She was just a person who'd befriended his daughter, and he apparently accepted that, within the next few days, she'd probably disappear back to London and away from their lives for ever.

But, it was something that he hadn't taken Ruth out for the day, she mused as they drove homeward later that afternoon. Or worse, she reflected. He could have suggested that Ruth came along with them!

She became aware that he was watching her as they neared the hotel.

When she glanced at him his gaze was upon her, although he was always watching the road while the car was travelling. Her heart went out to him. He deserved happiness, and she didn't think he would find it with Ruth.

'Well,' he said as they entered the hotel carpark. 'This is your last day as Mandy's mentor, Valerie. Miss Cannell will take over tomorrow, and I want to tell you how much I appreciate what you've done for Mandy. But it hasn't been much of a holiday for you! And I don't know how to repay you.'

'There's nothing to repay,' Valerie said quietly, glancing at Mandy, who was sitting passively on the back seat, with misery on her face. 'You'll be a good girl and work with Miss Cannell, won't you, Mandy?'

'I'd rather have you,' the girl replied. 'When are you going back to London?'

'Yes, what's going to happen now, Valerie?' Bruce demanded. 'You haven't said a word all week about your plans. We're interested in you, so why are you keeping it all a big secret?'

'I haven't made any plans,' Valerie protested. 'But it is time to sort out something, I agree. Now that Miss Cannell is taking over I'd better go back to my bungalow, hadn't I?'

'That depends on you.' Bruce shrugged. 'When are you going back to London? Have you decided yet?'

'Not really.' Valerie couldn't say that she wished she didn't have to go back at all. 'I spoke to my father the other night,' she added, 'and he's told me to take at least two more weeks.'

'Don't go home,' Mandy urged as they alighted from the car. 'Aren't you happier here than in London?'

'Now, that's what I call hitting the nail on the head,' Valerie observed, trying to lighten the situation. 'I have been happier here, but that's always the case, Mandy, when you're on holiday. I do have a job back home and I'll have to be going back soon. But I think I can quite safely stay on until you've had a chance to settle down with Miss Cannell.'

They walked to the hotel, and Valerie caught her breath as Bruce took hold of her elbow when they ascended the steps. Then her gaze picked out a face in the foyer that was very familiar, and a stab of shock cut through her daydreaming. The next moment, Robert was rising from a seat and advancing toward her, a triumphant smile upon his determined face.

7

'Well there you are!' Robert said, smiling triumphantly as Valerie stared at him in shocked amazement. 'Sorry for dropping in on you unannounced, but you didn't leave a forwarding address and you've stayed away far too long. I just had to see you.'

'I don't believe this!' Valerie gasped, glancing at Bruce, who was obviously studying Robert. 'Let me introduce you two. Bruce! Robert!' She paused as they shook hands.

'How do you do?' Bruce said. 'Excuse me and I'll take Mandy in to tea.' He nodded at Robert and smiled at Valerie. 'Come along, Mandy. Let's go for something to eat.'

Mandy gazed fearfully at Valerie, and stared at Robert as if he were a deadly enemy. Valerie watched Bruce lead the girl across the foyer, a sigh escaping her. Robert was the last person she needed to see at this moment, and she regarded him impatiently.

'How did you find me?' she demanded.

'It was easy. I recalled that your father bought a holiday place last year, and I found the address of the bungalow and this hotel in our old diary. When I arrived I checked the bungalow, found it locked, and came on here. The receptionist told me you were staying here.

'So this is where you've been hiding! And it seems as if you've made new friends. Who are those people?'

'I won't go into details now,' she responded. 'And I wish you hadn't come.' She looked into his face, and her heart seemed to cringe.

'I've allowed myself the week to bring you to your senses,' he said smoothly. 'We had a lot going for us, you know. And you don't have to worry about our friends. I've kept this business quiet. Nobody knows that you've come away because you got up-tight.'

'I didn't get up-tight about anything,' she retorted. 'And why ignore my decision? I've told you quite plainly that I have no intention of marrying you, and the sooner you accept that the better for both of us. I will not be changing my mind. So you'd be best going back to London.'

He smiled and shook his head, and Valerie realised that he wasn't even listening.

'Have you booked into the hotel?' she asked impatiently.

He nodded. 'I'm staying until tomorrow afternoon.'

'I'm sorry you've had all this trouble for nothing. You're wasting your time, Robert.'

'All I want is the opportunity to talk to you,' he said obstinately. 'Is that asking too much?'

'You'd realise it is if you could only read my mind,' she retorted. 'Why don't you ever accept my decision, Robert? No matter what I've suggested since we first met, you've always gone ahead without ever considering any of them. But this time you will listen. We're through, and I'll never come back to you. Can't you accept that?'

'You should give yourself time to think,' he retorted brusquely.

Valerie stared at him, noting the obstinate set of his jaw, and fought down the frustration that threatened to overwhelm her.

'It's useless trying to reason with you,' she observed, 'so if you'll excuse me I'll go on about my business. I'm taking care of the little girl you saw me with, and I'll be busy with her all day tomorrow.'

She turned away but he grasped her elbow, his face harshly set.

'I'm not leaving until I've come to some arrangement with you, Val. So it's no use trying to pretend that a relationship didn't exist between us. It's obvious now that some slight differences have arisen, but there's nothing that a bit of straight talking can't settle.'

Valerie sighed and turned away,

thankful that he made no attempt to follow her. She peeped into the dining-room and saw Bruce and Mandy eating tea at a corner table. Crossing to them, she paused beside Mandy's chair. Bruce looked up and smiled. At that moment she realised just how much she'd fallen in love with him.

'I'm sorry about the incident in the lobby,' she said uneasily. 'I didn't think Robert could track me down.'

'And now that he has?' Bruce countered.

'Are you going back to London, or will you stay here?' Mandy interrupted, her eyes looking as if they were fighting a losing battle against tears.

Valerie compressed her lips. Robert's arrival was ill-timed, to say the least, but she'd no intention of being panicked into any decision.

'I won't be going home for at least two more weeks,' she said.

Mandy chuckled and her eyes brightened. Valerie smiled, and suddenly she felt all right again. She saw Bruce's face relax slightly, and wondered if he cared that she was staying on.

'Robert has booked in until tomorrow,' she explained. 'I expect he'll leave just after lunch.'

'You don't like him, do you, Valerie?' Mandy asked as Valerie sat down beside her.

'I don't dislike him,' Valerie responded. 'It's just that I don't want to marry him, and he thinks I don't know my own mind. But he'll get the message eventually. I'll make sure of that.'

After tea, she and Mandy took Rajah for a walk in the cove, and almost bumped into Robert in the lobby. He was apparently intent upon enjoying Valerie's company, but they slipped by him leaving via the kitchen. When they reached the cove, Rajah went bounding off to do some exploring on his own and Mandy gave vent to a series of high-pitched yells in an attempt to relieve her tension.

It wasn't until Rajah began to bark that Valerie became aware of impending danger. Distracted from her own thoughts, she frowned as she gazed around to discover a reason for Rajah's behaviour. Then horror stabbed through her, for she saw that the tide was rushing into the cove and they were in the process of being cut off.

'Come on, Mandy, we must run for it,' she said instantly.

The advancing line of breakers had already cut off the yellow strand of beach that led around the headland, and they were at least half a mile from safety. As they ran hand in hand, Valerie blamed herself for not keeping an eye on the tide.

'Are there any other paths leading up to the cliffs, Mandy?' she asked, when they paused to get their breath. 'We're not going to reach the hotel path before the water cuts us off.'

Mandy shook her head. 'The only other path leads up to your bungalow, and that's already cut off.'

Valerie grasped Mandy's hand more tightly and they ran on again, with

Rajah dashing ahead. They were forced by the encroaching tide to stay close to the foot of the cliffs, which had never looked so high or so hostile. Valerie recalled how the beach was completely covered by water at high tide, and she began to look for a place where they might climb above the high-water mark. Rajah kept running back to them and barking, as if trying to spur them on to greater effort.

'Send Rajah home,' Valerie said when Mandy fell and they had to stop. 'Tell him to fetch your daddy, Mandy.'

'Rajah!' Mandy shouted tensely. 'Go home, boy. Fetch Daddy. Go and fetch Daddy!'

Rajah paused and stared at them, then turned his head and looked towards the path. He barked, before swinging around to dash off at top speed. Valerie lifted Mandy before hurrying on breathlessly until the rising water barred their progress, and they were still some two hundred yards from the foot of the hotel path. It didn't look very far, but the water was choppy, the incoming tide strong. It all looked very menacing.

Even while Valerie paused to take stock of the situation the rushing waves drew closer and spray flew into their faces.

'I'm frightened, Valerie,' Mandy said. 'My mummy drowned in this cove.'

Valerie compressed her lips as she visualised the beach at low tide. She shook her head, realising that the foot of the hotel path lay in a depression. Consequently, the water would be deeper there.

'What can we do, Valerie?' Mandy asked.

'It'll be all right.' Valerie spoke confidently, although an icy fear was clutching at her breast. 'Rajah has swum through the water and he's gone up the path. I can hear him barking on the cliff top. It's a pity he couldn't have taken you with him.'

'I wouldn't leave you,' Mandy declared stoutly.

Valerie smiled despite her misgiving. 'I think we should try and get to the path, Mandy. The tide is coming in extremely fast, and if we wait for your daddy we could be in much deeper water.'

'Daddy's always said that if I ever got cut off by the tide I should climb above high water and wait to be rescued,' Mandy said.

Valerie glanced around at the tall cliffs. Along this section of the cove they looked unscalable, and she did not think they would be able to ascend high enough to be safe.

'We must do something now,' she said grimly. 'Come on, I'll carry you. The water will come up to my shoulders, I think, but I'm a good swimmer so you needn't be frightened. Are you ready?'

Mandy nodded. Her face was pale. Valerie picked her up and walked into the water. It felt unusually cold, and she suppressed a shiver as she began to wade toward the foot of the path.

But before she had gone many yards she was out of her depth, and paused to look at Mandy, who was clinging to her in silent fear.

'We're going to have to swim from this point,' Valerie said reassuringly.

'But I can't swim!' Mandy gasped.

'Don't worry. I can swim well enough for both of us. I'm going to do the back stroke, and I'll put my hand under your chin and tow you. Breathe through your nose and don't panic. We'll be on the path in a few moments.'

She turned immediately and struck out. The tide helped, pushing them toward the cliff. Valerie swam strongly, worried for Mandy. She dimly heard a voice shouting in the background but did not pause beyond checking her direction. The path drew imperceptibly nearer, and for a moment she trod water and spoke to Mandy.

'Are you all right, Mandy?' she demanded.

'Yes,' came the frightened reply. 'Are we nearly there?'

'Not far now. Soon be on dry land.' Valerie struck out again, and moments later they were within reach of the path.

It was then that Valerie saw movement on the path, and relief filled her when she recognised Bruce, with Rajah at his side. Bruce was calling gentle encouragement, and Valerie pushed Mandy around so that he could grasp her. Bruce lifted Mandy clear of the water and Valerie hauled herself on to the path. She was exhausted.

'Are you all right?' Bruce demanded, holding Mandy in his arms and staring at Valerie. His face was stiff with tension.

'I'm fine,' Valerie replied. 'What about you, Mandy?'

'I'm all right,' the girl said shakily. 'I wasn't frightened, Valerie. I knew you wouldn't let anything bad happen to me.'

'Thank goodness I spotted the tide coming in when I did,' Valerie observed.

'You were very fortunate.' Bruce's voice was harsh with concern. 'And thank goodness you're such a strong swimmer! But let's get you both up to the hotel. A hot bath is what you need right now.'

Valerie felt guilty as they made their way to the hotel, and they aroused some interest when it became apparent that Valerie's clothes were wet. But Bruce led them up the stairs, and began to run a hot bath for Mandy while Valerie stripped off the girl's wet clothes.

'That was exciting,' Mandy commented as Valerie took her into the bathroom.

'I wouldn't want to go through it again,' Valerie retorted. There was a knot of cold shock in her stomach, and when she caught a glimpse of her reflection in a mirror she saw that her face was quite pale.

'Valerie, you'd better go and get out of your wet clothes,' Bruce ordered as he lifted Mandy into the bath. 'Put on your dressing-gown and come along to my bathroom. I'll run the bath for you.

Be quick. Mandy, you soak in that hot water until I come back to you.'

Valerie felt like a naughty schoolgirl as she went to her room. Stripping off her wet clothes, she pulled on her dressing-gown and pushed her feet into slippers. Then she went along the corridor to Bruce's bathroom, where he was busy running a bath for her.

'Soon be ready,' he commented, looking closely at her. 'Are you feeling all right? You look pale. It must have been quite an experience.'

'It wasn't too bad for me,' she replied. 'I've swum in much worse conditions. I was more worried about Mandy than anything else.'

'You coped very well. When I reached the top of the cliff and saw you and Mandy cut off I feared the worst. But, by the time I got to the foot of the path, you were swimming, and I could see that there was nothing to worry about. I would have dived in if I'd thought there was the slightest risk. But you must be very careful in future.'

'Don't worry, I won't get caught out again,' Valerie promised.

Bruce nodded and withdrew, and Valerie thankfully stepped into the bath. She felt better as the hot water chased out the cold from her body, and she began to relax. The hot water soothed her nerves also.

By the time she'd dressed, Valerie felt much better. She went along to Mandy's room to find the girl playing with Bruce, and they both looked up at her entrance and smiled.

'That's better,' Bruce said. 'I'll bet you feel good now, don't you?'

'I do, thanks.' Valerie nodded. 'What about you, Mandy? Are you feeling all right?'

'Yes, thank you. It was a bit cold for swimming, but Daddy says when the weather gets warmer he'll teach me to swim.' Mandy paused and studied Valerie for a moment. 'If you didn't go back to London you could stay here with us, and teach me to swim when the summer comes.'

'Mandy,' Bruce warned. He got to his feet. 'Can I leave you two now?' he asked. 'I'll be in the office. I have some letters to write.'

'What shall we do?' Valerie asked Mandy as Bruce departed. 'We have an hour before you have to go to bed.'

'Let's go for a walk,' Mandy suggested. 'We've been sitting in Daddy's car most of the day.'

They went down to the lobby, and Robert appeared from nowhere, a grim expression on his face.

'Were you trying to commit suicide, Val?' he demanded. 'I heard what happened. Don't you think it's time to stop playing games and start thinking seriously about the future? I wish I knew what had got in to you! Your behaviour is most odd.'

'I wish I could make you accept my decision,' she retorted. Her eyes narrowed when Ruth suddenly appeared in the doorway and came striding towards the reception desk. 'You'll have to excuse me,' Valerie said hurriedly. 'I must take

Mandy for a walk.'

Ruth passed them without greeting, and Valerie frowned as she led Mandy out of the hotel. They walked along the top of the cliffs, and Valerie suppressed a shiver when she looked down and saw that the entire cove was under water. They'd had a narrow escape.

'What would have happened if you couldn't swim, Valerie?' Mandy asked.

'Someone would have spotted us and sent the rescue people to save us,' Valerie replied.

'Like we saw in the display at Land's End?'

'That's right.' Valerie smiled. 'We had a nice day there, didn't we? I'll miss Cornwall when I have to go back to London.'

'Do you have to go back?' Mandy countered.

'Yes, when the time comes.' Valerie knew that she had to be firm. 'You know, Mandy, there are lots of times in life when you have to do things that you don't really like, and for me this is one of them.'

'Does that mean you'll go back and marry Robert?'

'No. I'll never marry Robert, and I wish he could see that. But he will get the message eventually, I expect.'

'Will you stay at the hotel until you finish your holiday?' Mandy's face was intent.

'Yes, I expect so. And one day you'll come to London to see me.' Valerie smiled.

'I'd like that,' Mandy said, her eyes shining.

They walked back to the hotel. Mandy was silent now. Daylight was beginning to fade. The sun had sunk low in the western part of the sky. Valerie felt a deep peace rise inside her. Leaving Cornwall would be a big wrench. She pictured Bruce's face, and wondered if she'd ever see him again once she'd returned to London.

As they crossed the hotel lobby, Valerie spotted Robert in the bar, and her heart gave a lurch when she saw that Ruth was sitting at the same table. Pausing, she stared into the smokey atmosphere, noting that Ruth was talking quite animatedly to Robert, whose face was glum.

She wondered where Bruce was, and saw him as she turned away. He was in the office, talking to Miss Harper. He glanced out the open door and his expression changed when he saw her and Mandy. Immediately he came striding out of his office into the foyer.

'Had a good walk?' he enquired, and Valerie noted that he was tense. He placed a hand on Mandy's head and smiled. 'You look very tired. You've had a very busy day, haven't you?' He glanced at Valerie. 'You look as if you're still suffering from shock. When you've seen Mandy to bed would you join me in the bar? You need something to relax you.'

'Oh! No, not in the bar!' she said quickly, not wanting to join Ruth and Robert.

When he stared at her uncompre-hendingly, she moistened her lips.

'I just spotted Robert in the bar and I have no wish to be in his company. I'd like to keep out of his way until he leaves tomorrow.'

Bruce nodded. 'I have to go into the bar,' he told her.

'Yes. I saw Ruth in there, getting very friendly with Robert!' She smiled.

Bruce shook his head and turned away, and Valerie felt dispirited as she and Mandy continued up the stairs.

When Mandy was in bed, Valerie went to her own room to change her dress. She wanted to be in Bruce's company so badly that she was willing to risk Robert's presence. But, when she reached the reception desk, she lost her nerve and went into the office instead.

'Hello, Valerie,' Miss Harper greeted. 'I've just been talking to Jim. Are you going to call him this evening?'

'I hadn't planned to,' Valerie replied. 'I have something here to sort out before I call home again.'

'Robert!' Miss Harper nodded. 'He's told me something of your troubles, although I didn't ask for it. He's quite upset, Valerie.'

'I know, but there's nothing I can do. I just can't make him listen to my side of it. I suppose what I ought to do is leave and give him time to get over it, or return home and let time sort it out.'

'Time takes care of most things,' Miss Harper said wisely.

Valerie nodded and smiled ruefully. Time was the one thing she did not have in abundance. In two weeks, at the most, she would be returning to London to slip back into the old routine, and any action she wanted to take concerning her future would have to be made before that time arrived, for afterwards, she knew only too well, would be too late!

8

On Sunday morning, Valerie took Mandy for a drive, intent upon staying away from the hotel until Robert had gone back to London. She felt miserable because Robert obviously cared for her and she didn't want to cause him any heartache. But she couldn't marry him at the expense of her own happiness! Robert would have to be made to accept that.

Mandy was rather quiet, Valerie realised when she surfaced from her own musing and glanced at the child, who was in the back seat.

'Are you worried about something, Mandy?' she asked softly, and the girl stirred and looked at her with troubled, brown eyes.

'It's Sunday and Miss Cannell arrives today.' Mandy sighed and shook her head. 'This is our last day together.'

Valerie forced a laugh. 'Well don't be so mournful,' she reproached lightly. 'You make it sound like the end of the world. But I'm not going home for another two weeks, and I'm staying on at the hotel.'

'But two weeks will soon go, and then you'll be gone! If you can't stay in Cornwall, why can't I come to London with you?'

Valerie sighed and gazed ahead. 'That wouldn't work out, dear,' she said. 'Who'd look after you? I have to work. And you'd miss your daddy.'

'We could try it and see if I do miss him!' Mandy ventured, and frowned when Valerie shook her head.

'Just think about your daddy for a moment,' Valerie said. 'He loves you, Mandy, and would miss you terribly if you went away. He misses your mother, and relies on you.'

'He's going to marry Ruth.' Mandy's voice quivered.

Valerie threw a glance at the girl, wondering if Mandy had heard something to that effect.

'What do you mean?' she asked softly. 'Has your daddy said he's going to marry Ruth?'

'Daddy hasn't said anything, but I heard Ruth talking to Robert last night. I went down to get some lemonade from the kitchen and heard them talking in the lobby. If Daddy does marry Ruth, could I come to live with you, Valerie? I don't want to stay here.'

Valerie shook her head. She could imagine how Mandy would get treated if Ruth became her stepmother. But she said nothing. Whatever Ruth had said to Robert, Bruce had not made up his mind about matrimony, of that Valerie was certain. And it was not her concern. She sighed as she parked the car in St Austell.

'We can look at the church before morning service begins,' she said, and they walked around the narrow streets.

All in all it was a rather bleak day, she considered as they drove homeward during the late afternoon. Although the

154

sun was shining and the weather was warm, there was a chill in her heart. She felt dispirited because she was truly in love for the first time in her life and the emotion was not reciprocated. They pulled into the hotel carpark, and Valerie sat for a moment, wondering if Robert had departed.

'There's Daddy!' Mandy cried as they got out of the car, and Valerie looked up with fast-beating heart to see Bruce emerging from the hotel with Ruth, who was holding his arm. 'Oh, Ruth is with him,' the girl observed. 'Let's go round this way, Valerie. I'd rather not see her.'

They circled the carpark and entered the hotel by a side door. It was tea-time, and Valerie insisted that they freshen up before eating. As they crossed the lobby, Miss Harper called from the office doorway, and Valerie turned on the bottom stair to see the manageress waving a letter.

'Robert left about two hours ago,' Miss Harper said, coming forward. 'He hung on as long as he could, but when he realised that you wouldn't be back he wrote to you.'

She handed over the letter.

'Thank you.' Valerie experienced a pang of guilt but forced her emotions into the background.

'I didn't think you'd be on duty today,' she observed. 'Do you work seven days a week, Miss Harper?'

The manageress smiled. 'Every other Sunday,' she said. 'Actually I should be off duty today but Mr Stirling has a business appointment so I'm standing in for him.'

'A business appointment on a Sunday?' Valerie shook her head. 'I've never heard of such a thing! Bruce certainly puts in some hours, doesn't he?'

'It's the new leisure complex he's working on.' Miss Harper leaned forward confidentially. 'There's a partner who lives in Bristol, and he can only get here for meetings at odd times.'

Valerie sighed as some of the tension

lifted from her. It pleased her to think that Bruce was going out on business and not pleasure, even though Ruth was with him!

'Has Miss Cannell arrived yet?' she asked, changing the subject.

'No.' Miss Harper glanced at the silent Mandy, who was holding Valerie's hand. 'She telephoned about an hour ago to say that she was visiting a friend in Plymouth before coming on to the hotel. So we can expect her later.'

Mandy tugged at Valerie's hand and they turned to the stairs. The girl was silent until they reached her room. Then she squeezed Valerie's hand. Valerie kneeled down and put her arms around the child.

'This isn't a very happy day,' Mandy said. 'I wish it was over.'

'I know what you mean.' Valerie smiled. 'But don't give up. Time passes, and you'll soon settle down to your new way of life. I wouldn't be surprised if you enjoyed things greatly. You should be very happy at the prospect of having a new governess.'

'Daddy said that if I wasn't happy with Miss Cannell then he would find someone else.'

'You must give Miss Cannell a chance, you know.' Valerie spoke firmly. 'She will be thinking only of your well-being, and if you do the very best you can then you'll be a lot happier.'

'I'll try my best,' Mandy promised.

'There's a good girl!' Valerie smiled.

'And you'll come and see me again?' Mandy pleaded.

'I will, I promise you,' Valerie replied.

After tea they took Rajah for a walk, paying a visit to the bungalow, and shadows were falling when they made their way back to the hotel. Mandy was tired, and Valerie was aware that they'd both be relieved when the day had ended. They hadn't enjoyed the day at all.

They reached the hotel to find Miss Cannell there, waiting to be introduced to Mandy. She was a tall, middle-aged woman with a slight Scottish accent, and Valerie liked her on sight. Mandy hung back a little, but Miss Cannell soon put her at ease, and suggested that she and Mandy have a chat together. Valerie stood at the reception desk as the two walked up the stairs to Mandy's room, and there was a great emotional tugging at her heart.

Bruce appeared at that moment, and Valerie straightened when she saw him, her spirits rising immediately. He was carrying a slim briefcase under one arm, and looked tired, she thought, as he came toward her. He smiled when he saw her and came to her side.

'Hello,' he greeted. 'Where's Mandy? I've got so used to seeing you two together that I feel something's wrong if you're alone. Have you had enough of her today? Has she gone to bed?'

'I've lost my job, I'm afraid.' Valerie forced a smile. 'Miss Cannell has arrived, and she and Mandy are getting acquainted.'

'So you're now at a loose end and feeling miserable,' he said.

'I beg your pardon?' She was startled.
He smiled. 'I can tell by your eyes.
You look positively downcast! Didn't
you have a good day?'

For a moment, Valerie feared she was
going to burst into tears. Bruce was
watching her closely, and reached out
and grasped her arm.

'You're depressed,' he observed sympathetically. 'Let me put my case in the
office, then we'll have a drink together.
We haven't had an opportunity to chat
for some time, and as Mandy has now
been taken off your hands, I think we
ought to make an effort to see that you
enjoy the remainder of your holiday. We
owe you that much.'

'That sounds intriguing,' she
ventured, and he chuckled and went
into the office to deposit the case. He
emerged from the office as Mandy
and Miss Cannell descended the
stairs, and Mandy came running to
greet him. He swung her into his
arms, shook hands with Miss Cannell,
and then kissed his daughter, eyes

bright as he gazed at Valerie.

'The last two weeks have been most eventful,' he said. 'When you came for the job interview, Miss Cannell, you remarked on Mandy's reactions to everyone around her. Now you must see a big difference in her — and it's all due to Valerie. I'm so deeply in her debt that I don't know how to repay her.'

'So that's it,' Miss Cannell remarked. 'I couldn't help noticing the change in Mandy.' She smiled at Valerie. 'You must love children very much.'

'I do, but I don't know what happened with Mandy!' Valerie smiled and reached out to touch Mandy's hair. Her hand brushed Bruce's cheek and she compressed her lips as he set Mandy down and patted the girl's head.

'I rather fancy that it's way past your bedtime, Mandy,' he observed. 'I want to talk to Valerie, so perhaps Miss Cannell will see you off to bed. There's a good girl now. Off you go.'

'Will you see her off to bed now, Miss

Cannell?' he said, turning towards the bar.

'Certainly,' the new governess responded, taking Mandy's hand. 'Kiss Valerie good-night, my dear.'

'Will you look in on me later, Valerie?' Mandy whispered as she kissed Valerie's cheek.

'Of course,' Valerie replied. 'I'll come and tuck you in.'

She sighed as Mandy departed with Miss Cannell. A weight seemed to lift from her mind as she realised that her responsibility had ended, and a sigh escaped her as Bruce took her elbow and led her to the bar.

'Now perhaps you can begin to enjoy your holiday,' he said as she sat down at a table. 'I've been watching you over the past two weeks. You looked after Mandy as if you were her mother! And you've worked wonders with her! How do I ever repay you, Valerie?'

She smiled. Her name sounded beautiful on his lips. 'There's nothing to repay,' she said firmly. 'I've thoroughly enjoyed every minute of the past fortnight.'

'I'll get us a drink,' he said, and turned to the bar.

Valerie leaned back in her seat, watching him, her thoughts sombre, a troubled expression upon her face. He came back and set a glass in front of her, smiling as he met her gaze.

'I haven't forgotten what you drink.' He sat opposite, sighing with relief as he relaxed. 'You know, it seems such a long time since we went to Land's End. And I enjoyed it so much! We must do it again before your holiday ends. It was a marvellous day! I felt alive for the first time since my wife died. I'd forgotten almost how to relax.'

There was a frown on his face as he spoke. Valerie caught her breath.

'I'm slowly coming back to normal,' he mused. 'And it's about time. It's been more than two years. You brought Mandy out of her grief, and helped me a great deal at the same time. Thank goodness I've been busy with this leisure park idea. It saved my sanity. But I'm still worried about Mandy.'

'I think Mandy has got over the worst of it now,' Valerie said. 'And I'll be around for another fortnight.'

'What she really needs is a stable home life.' He spoke grimly, gazing at the amber liquid in his glass. His hand was tense, Valerie noted, the knuckles white around the glass. 'Living here in the hotel is not the same as living in a house,' he continued. 'And Mandy needs a woman's attention. Not a companion but someone she can look upon as a mother. How do you think she would react to a stepmother, Valerie?'

'That would depend on how the stepmother handled her,' Valerie replied, thinking of Ruth. 'The wrong handling could actually set her back to exactly where she was before.'

'Yes, that's what I'm thinking.' He sipped his drink, and for a moment his eyes were upon her.

Valerie felt her face grow warm. If it

was possible, she'd apply for the job of Mandy's stepmother but she knew that was merely wishful thinking.

'Would you like another drink?' he asked, and Valerie glanced down at her glass to find that she'd drained it.

'No thanks. One is quite sufficient.' She tried to find the words to tell him not to worry about Mandy, but words would not come, as she gazed at him, hopelessly in love and tongue-tied.

'Did you see Robert before he checked out?' he asked, and she shook her head.

'No. I stayed out on purpose so that I wouldn't have to see him again. He shouldn't have come, really.'

'Did your father give him your whereabouts?'

'No.' She shook her head emphatically. 'Dad wouldn't do that! Robert played a hunch and it came off.'

Miss Harper appeared at the table, smiling apologetically.

'Sorry to interrupt,' she said, 'but you're wanted on the telephone, Bruce.'

He frowned, then shrugged fatalistically and arose. 'Excuse me, Valerie,' he apologised. 'I won't be a moment.'

She tried to relax as he departed, but her mind teemed with conjecture. Miss Harper paused for a moment.

'Mandy has to face up to reality again,' she observed. 'The next few days will be crucial for her.'

'Yes. We were just discussing the situation.' Valerie nodded. 'I'm staying on for another two weeks, so if there's anything I can do, well, I'll be on hand. But I'm sure everyrhting will be OK.'

Miss Harper nodded and turned away. Then she paused and glanced back at Valerie.

'You were the best thing that happened around here in many a long year,' she said seriously. 'I wish you luck whatever you do.'

'Thank you!' Valerie smiled. But as Miss Harper departed, her face sobered. She looked at the letter which Robert had written her. Opening it, she discovered that it merely reiterated everything he'd said. A pang of impatience cut her and she screwed up the letter in frustration.

Bruce returned shaking his head. 'I have to be in London first thing in the morning,' he said. 'That means getting some papers together now and leaving as soon as possible.' He sighed. 'I'll be glad when these negotiations are finished. I'm sorry, Valerie. I was enjoying our little chat. I'd like the chance to speak with you again. But I'll see you when I get back.'

'Certainly.' She smiled, but her heart felt as if it were breaking as she arose to go to her room.

That night sleep did not come easily, and Valerie tossed and turned. Eventually she did slumber, but not deeply, and several times she awoke and half sat up, peering around in the gloom. When morning came she arose early to bathe and dress, before slipping quietly out of the hotel to take a walk along the cliffs. The fresh air might make her feel a little better.

The day stretched unbroken before her. Now that Miss Cannell was here she would not have Mandy for company, and realised, with some surprise, that she really missed her! For the past two weeks she'd been concerned about Mandy's feelings when the time for parting came, but she hadn't expected to feel such a wrench herself.

She went to the bungalow and threw herself into cleaning it right through. She dusted, polished, washed all the crockery, cleaned the windows, and when she'd finished it was still only ten-thirty. Making herself a cup of tea, she sat down to drink it, but the telephone rang as she tried to relax. She picked up the receiver and an emotional voice spoke in her ear.

'Valerie, is that you? Thank goodness! This is Tom Aitken. I'm calling from the Gordon Harrington hospital. We've just brought your father here. He'd an accident in the garage.'

Valerie froze in horror.

'Dad's hurt?' she demanded. 'Oh, Tom! Is it bad?'

'It's too soon to say, Val. They're looking at him now. I'll call you back as soon as I learn something.'

'Do you have the number of the hotel where I'm staying?' she asked. It seemed to her shocked mind that her voice belonged to another.

'No. I called the bungalow because I thought that's where you're staying.'

'I'm at a hotel about a mile from the bungalow. My car is there. While we're waiting for news I'll go to the hotel and stand by. If you learn anything before I get there then leave a message for me. I'll pack and be ready to come home immediately we know something definite.'

'OK, Val, and try not to worry.'

The line went dead and Valerie replaced the receiver, her hands cold and trembling. Her mind whirled with conjecture, and she could only think the worst . . .

By the time she reached the hotel her

nerves were overstretched. Tears streamed down her face. When she entered the office, Miss Harper looked up, and then sprang to her feet.

'Valerie, what on earth is wrong?' she gasped.

Valerie began to explain. Miss Harper listened and then made her sit down. She called the kitchen and asked for a pot of strong tea.

'There hasn't been a call yet,' she said as she poured Valerie a cup of tea. 'You'll certainly have to go home. What a shame that Bruce isn't here! You shouldn't travel alone.'

'I'll be all right,' Valerie insisted, sipping the tea. 'I'd better go and pack. I'll have to leave as soon as I get word.' She stood up. 'I'll be up in my room, Miss Harper. Call me if you hear anything.'

Valerie went to the door, paused and looked back at the sympathetic manageress.

'Where's Mandy?' she asked.

'She's taken Miss Cannell on a

sight-seeing tour of the area.'

'Does Mandy seem happy?'

'Yes, I think so, although you can never tell with that one. But don't worry about her, Valerie. I'm sure she'll be all right. Now go and pack. I'll call you the minute I hear something.'

Valerie nodded and went up to her room, her mind in turmoil. Having packed, she carried the cases down to the lobby, and was setting them down when Miss Harper appeared in the office doorway.

'Valerie, I've just heard.' Miss Harper's face was grimly set.

Valerie hurried to the office, hands clenched.

'There's nothing broken,' Miss Harper said consolingly. 'He's very badly bruised, and concussed, and because he was knocked unconscious they're keeping him in for observation.'

Valerie drew a deep breath. Then she sighed raggedly. Perhaps it wasn't too bad after all! She fought against tears.

'I must go home,' she said, 'and I'd

better leave right away.'

'Will you be all right?' Miss Harper was worried. 'You've had quite a shock. Is it safe for you to drive?'

'I'll manage,' Valerie replied. 'Give my love to Mandy, and please tell Bruce what's happened.'

'I certainly will, and give my best regards to your father when you see him.' Miss Harper shook her head sadly. 'Tell him I hope he'll soon get better.'

Valerie turned away. There was no time to think of Mandy or the man she loved. She carried her cases out to the car, put them in the boot, and was about to get into the driving-seat when Ruth Ordway spoke to her.

'Leaving, Valerie?' the woman demanded, and Valerie turned quickly, for Ruth had approached silently, surprising her. 'I understood that you were staying another two weeks. Have you had second thoughts about Robert? Such a nice young man! I had quite a chat with him before he left. But I expect you'll be coming this way again, if only to see how Mandy is getting on. You may even get an invitation to the wedding.'

'Wedding?' Valerie frowned. 'What wedding?'

Ruth gazed at her for a moment before chuckling. 'The wedding of the year,' she retorted, turning away.

Valerie stared after Ruth, her mind filled with concern for her father. She couldn't comprehend Ruth's words as she slid into the driving seat and started the engine. Then she began the long drive to London . . .

9

Valerie did not remember much of that nightmarish drive to London. She was hardly aware of the journey and afterwards only remembered parking at the hospital. Alighting stiffly, she walked towards the main entrance, her legs trembling.

But visitors were leaving as she entered, and the receptionist informed her that visiting was over for the day. Valerie leaned on the desk, her legs trembling. She had reached breaking point, and felt like weeping.

'Valerie!' A voice spoke at her back and she turned to see Robert, his face grim. 'So you got here at last!' he said.

'What are you doing here?' she countered.

'I heard about your father's accident and knew you were in Cornwall so I came along.'

'I'm too late to see him,' she said harshly. 'How is he?'

'Not seriously hurt. He was badly concussed.'

'But is he all right?' she demanded.

'His life isn't in any danger.' Robert spoke sharply, frowning as he stared at her. 'He's very badly shocked. You haven't driven all the way from Cornwall under the impression that he might be dying, have you?'

She nodded helplessly, filled with an overwhelming relief. Tears ran down her cheeks and she trembled. Then weakness seized her. She swayed and would have fallen, if Robert hadn't held her tightly. She closed her eyes and clung to him, sobbing as reaction set in.

'I'd better take you home,' he said gruffly. 'Didn't you stop on the way to get something to eat?'

She shook her head wordlessly, and pulled against him when he started to lead her toward the exit.

'There's nothing you can do here,' he remonstrated. 'Your father is asleep.

He's comfortable. That's all they'll tell you. So, let me see you home. You look all in.'

Valerie was on the point of collapse, and gave no further resistance. Robert kept a supporting arm around her as they went out to the carpark.

'My car's over there,' she said, but he shook his head.

'You're in no fit condition to drive. I'll take you home. My car's this way. You can pick up yours in the morning.'

She didn't argue, and sat slumped, with her eyes closed, as he drove her home. When they arrived she'd difficulty in getting out of the car, and Robert helped her. He held her upright while she fumbled in her bag for the front-door key. Darkness had closed in and Valerie felt ill, and faint with hunger. There was a nagging pain behind her eyes and her head ached with a sickening throb that made her long for the blessed oblivion of sleep.

'I'll come in and get you some food,'

Robert said. 'You're practically on your knees, Val.'

'I'll be all right,' she protested. 'I can manage, thank you.'

'Are you home for good?' He grasped her arm, holding her motionless on the doorstep.

'I've no idea!' She tried to summon up whatever strength she had left. 'I must go in. Thank you for bringing me home.'

He had to let her go. She locked the door thankfully, then sagged weakly against it. Switching on the light, she forced herself to go into the kitchen, and ate some bread and butter while waiting for the kettle to boil. After she'd eaten she felt better, but was utterly exhausted. She showered and then tumbled thankfully into bed.

When she awoke next morning her headache had gone, and she lay motionless, recollecting her scattered wits. When she remembered, the knowledge was sufficient to drive her out of bed, and she saw that the time was almost nine. Pulling on a dressing-gown, she hurried down to the hall to telephone the hospital.

Tears of relief flowed when she learned that Jim had spent a comfortable night and was recovering from shock. She'd be able to visit him that afternoon. After breakfast, she called Miss Harper at the hotel, her pulses racing as she pictured the scene there.

'Hello, it's Valerie,' she said when she heard a voice at the other end of the line.

'Valerie! I'm so pleased you called. How's your father?'

Valerie explained, and Miss Harper gave vent to her relief.

'I telephoned Bruce yesterday after-noon,' the manageress said, 'and told him what had happened. He said he'd try to get in touch with you. Hasn't he done so yet?'

'No.' Valerie frowned.

Now that her apprehension had gone she was able to think more rationally, and Ruth's parting words returned to her mind. What had the woman meant by saying that she might get an invitation to the wedding? She gave up trying to unravel the riddle, and asked Miss Harper about Mandy.

'She's doing very well, Valerie. Better than I hoped. But it was your influence that put her on the right track. She's having some lessons this morning, and that's something I haven't seen in a very long time.'

'Remember me to her, will you?' Valerie asked. 'I miss her very much.'

'We're going to miss you around here,' Miss Harper responded.

They chatted until Miss Harper had to ring off, and Valerie promised to call again next day. Then she hung up and sat back, picturing Bruce, wondering where he was in London and why he hadn't contacted her.

She went to the garage, sat down to work, and kept busy for the rest of the morning. She looked at the inspection pit into which her father had fallen, and heard the details of the accident from the mechanics.

Just before lunch-time, Robert walked into the office, and she sat back at the desk and studied him with unblinking gaze.

'It's lunch-time,' he greeted, 'and I thought we could have something to eat together. I want to ensure that you eat something.'

'I don't have time to stop right now,' she replied. 'I'm going to the hospital this afternoon, and want everything sorted out here before I see my father. I'll stay on here.'

'I'll get something and bring it back for you,' he said.

'Robert, I appreciate your concern, but please don't,' she said in a determined tone. 'And please don't come to see me again. You know how I feel about our relationship, and it will be better if we maintain the clean break I've spent two weeks making.'

'You can't blame a man for trying,' he retorted. 'And what happened down in Cornwall? Did you fall in love with that hotelier?'

She thought of Bruce and wished she could see him. If only he'd call!

'Nothing happened in Cornwall,' she retorted. 'And, really, it's none of your business, Robert.'

He stared at her for a moment, then smiled enigmatically and departed. Valerie promptly dismissed him from her mind and resumed working.

At two-thirty she walked into the hospital, eager to see her father. When she entered his ward and saw him her heart missed a beat. He spotted her and smiled, lifting a hand in greeting, as she ran to the bedside. His head was bandaged, his face ashen.

'Dad!' She dropped to her knees at his side and hugged him, then kissed his cheek. When she looked more closely at him she saw that he seemed years older. 'What on earth have you been up to?' she demanded. 'Can't I go away for two weeks without you trying something?'

'It was just one of those things,' he said weakly. 'No-one's fault. I mis-judged my position in relation to the pit. But not to worry. I'm not hurt. Shook up, that's all. Nothing's broken, and they'll probably discharge me tomorrow. When did you come back?'

'Yesterday. Tom rang me at the bungalow after you'd been brought here and I started back immediately, arriving here as visiting time ended.'

'I'm sorry to have interrupted your holiday,' he said faintly. 'But I'm all right now, so you can get into your car and drive back to Cornwall.'

Valerie was faintly surprised by his words, and he grinned as he met her gaze.

'It's all right,' he said. 'My mind wasn't damaged in that fall yesterday. I know how important Cornwall is to you right now. So don't worry about me. Go back to where you came from and everything will be all right.'

'I'm not going anywhere,' she asserted. 'Who's going to run the garage while you're unfit? You've been letting the paperwork slide as it is. I spent all morning trying to bring it up to date.'

'You worry too much!' He fingered his bandage. 'There's a time and place for everything, and you should go back to Cornwall.'

She refused to pursue the subject further. He studied her intently for a moment and then sighed.

'Your stay in Cornwall has done you a lot of good,' he remarked. 'You're not looking harassed any more. Have you got Robert off your mind?'

She told him of Robert's arrival in Cornwall, and he nodded, lips pursed.

'That was probaby to the good,' he remarked. 'If he's got the message you'll be able to settle down and start remaking your life. Are you coming back to the garage to take up where you left off?'

She frowned. 'I don't understand, Dad! Why should there be any question about my future?'

'It happens sometimes.' He shrugged. 'You may feel that it's time to make a change.' He paused, then asked. 'You got very friendly with the Stirlings, didn't you?'

'With Mandy,' she countered.

'What about Bruce?' His gaze was steady.

'What about him?' She had to force herself to speak casually.

'You'll probably get married one day, and Bruce Stirling is the kind of man you should go for!'

Valerie chuckled, but the sound did not sound natural, and she wondered if she could fool her father.

But he changed the subject, went on to talk about the garage and what needed to be done during the next few days. Then visiting time was over and she departed, to return to the garage and continue with the paperwork.

She called Miss Harper and passed on the word of her father's condition.

'I'm so glad,' the manageress said. 'I'll tell Bruce when he gets home.

Didn't you see him?'

'No.' Valerie was disappointed.

'He did say that he was extremely busy.' Miss Harper's voice suddenly sounded faint, and there was a crackling on the telephone. 'But no doubt he'll call you when he gets home. I think he's coming back today.'

Valerie heard the door of the office open and glanced around to see Robert entering.

'I have to go now, Miss Harper,' she said. 'Give my love to Mandy. I'd love to talk to her on the phone, if it's possible.'

'I'll see what I can do the next time you call,' Miss Harper promised.

Valerie hung up and turned to face Robert, who dropped into the chair beside the desk.

'I came to find out how your father is,' he said.

Valerie told him. He nodded, and she suspected that he was feeling very pleased with himself for some reason or other. The petulance he had been experiencing because she'd rejected his proposal seemed to have evaporated. He was looking rather smug.

'Calling Cornwall, were you?' he asked. 'Strange how you got so involved with that girl. Or was it the father you became interested in? I hope it wasn't, because he and Ruth Ordway are secretly engaged. They're just waiting for his leisure park plans to be settled before coming into the open and making arrangements for their marriage.'

Valerie stiffened at his words, and clenched her teeth against the protest that arose in her mind. No, she thought. Not that! Ruth was not right for Bruce, and certainly wrong for Mandy.

'I had several little chats with Ruth while I was there over the week-end,' Robert went on smoothly. 'She thought you were falling in love with Bruce, and was on the point of warning you off, but I told her that you couldn't possibly be in love with him. I know you, Val.

And whatever you are, you wouldn't fall for his type.'

Valerie caught her breath, stunned by the revelation. But she struggled to keep her face expressionless. 'I don't know about you,' she said lightly, 'but I have a lot of work to do, so if you'll excuse me!' She turned back to the desk and pretended to resume working.

'I really dropped by to ask if I could see you this evening.' There was sudden tension in his voice.

'No.' She spoke without looking up. 'It's all over, Robert, and the sooner you accept that the better.'

She kept on working, and a moment later heard the door close softly. When she looked round, he'd gone.

Valerie sighed and leaned back in her seat. Ruth and Bruce secretly engaged! She recalled the large diamond ring that Ruth wore, and a bitter sigh escaped her. So that was it! That was why Bruce had always looked impersonally at her.

She recalled her own torrid feelings

for Bruce, and her face burned with embarrassment. Supposing he'd recognised her emotions for what they were! Then she thought of Mandy, and hopelessness filled her. If that was the situation then she couldn't return to Cornwall. But Mandy would soon forget her if she didn't contact the hotel again. The girl would become engrossed with her new life, although Valerie couldn't imagine what kind of a life Ruth would give the girl.

The shock of her father's accident and the hurt of the revelation that Robert had delivered was altogether too much for Valerie's peace of mind. But hard work seemed to be an antidote for what ailed her and she forced herself to concentrate upon the office routine.

Two days passed during which Valerie didn't call Miss Harper, and she was surprised when the woman didn't ring to ask about Jim. But there was complete silence, and, on the afternoon of the second day, Valerie took her father's clothes to the hospital, and then drove him home.

Jim took her on a tour of the garage when they reached it, as if he'd been afraid that he would never see it again. Then they went home, and he grumbled when Valerie insisted that he rest.

That evening Jim switched off the TV set and glanced across at Valerie, who was reading. He moistened his lips, opened his mouth to speak, then decided against it. Valerie glanced up at him, sensing that he was uneasy about something.

'What's wrong, Dad?' she enquired.

'I'm all right.' He shrugged. 'Just feeling unsettled.' He paused, and then went on, 'Do you know what I'd like to do?'

'No.' She shook her head. 'Why don't you tell me?'

'I'd like to go down to the bungalow for a few days. I think I need a complete change of scenery.'

'That sounds like a good idea,' she agreed. 'Why don't you drive down tomorrow and stay the week? I found it really bracing.'

'The doctor at the hospital told me I shouldn't drive for at least another week.'

He was examining his fingernails intently. 'Would you drive me?'

'Someone's got to take care of the office,' she pointed out, frowning.

'It wouldn't matter for one day,' he pressed. 'You could stay at the bungalow overnight and return here next morning. Then you could come down next week and pick me up. By then I should be as right as rain!' He smiled. 'The doctor did say that a change of scenery would be beneficial,' he added.

'All right, I'll drive you down tomorrow if you think you can stand the trip. But I won't be staying!'

'That's all right.' He nodded. 'You live your life and I'll live mine.'

Valerie agreed, and next morning found herself driving to Cornwall once more.

It was late afternoon when they reached the bungalow, and Jim staggered as he alighted from the car.

Valerie hurried to his side but he waved her away.

'I'm all right,' he said sharply. 'Just stiff from the drive. I've got a bit of a headache so I think I'll take a tablet and lie down. If you don't make any noise around the place I might be able to get some sleep.'

'I shan't make any noise,' Valerie retorted, dragging the cases out of the car. 'As soon as you lie down I'll go for a walk.'

'Sorry,' he said. 'I didn't mean to sound grumpy. But I'm not used to these headaches I'm getting. The doctor did say that they'll ease off in a couple of days so I'll just have to grin and bear it.'

Valerie understood, and said so, and as soon as her father went to lie down she departed to walk to the cove.

As she descended the cliff path below the bungalow she thought of the first time she'd come this way, when Rajah had confronted her and Bruce had been rather harsh. Then had followed those happy days with Mandy! Her heart ached under the strain of knowing that it was all over. How could Bruce fall in love with a woman like Ruth? And how was poor Mandy faring now?

She walked along the shore in the direction of the hotel, recalling how she and Mandy had been cut off by the tide. The thought made her check the tidal situation, and she caught her breath when two distant figures attracted her gaze. Narrowing her eyes, she was startled to see that they were Bruce and Mandy, obviously out for a walk.

Her first reaction was to run, but she realised that if she did they'd see her. Turning to the left, she hurried toward a large cluster of rocks, and sought the shelter of their cover. Her heart was pounding as she crouched behind a rock and peered out to see where Mandy and Bruce were.

They were walking straight towards the rocks! Valerie gasped and moved deeper into the cluster. Her heart ached when Mandy's voice rang out as it had done when they'd been together. She closed her eyes, hoping that they would quickly turn and retrace their steps to the distant hotel.

But Mandy stopped only feet away from the rocks and picked up a stick to write in the sand. Valerie craned forward to get a good look at the girl, wondering why she was not with her new governess.

'What do you think Valerie's doing now?' Mandy asked. 'I wish she was my governess instead of Miss Cannell. Why didn't you ask her to stay with me, Daddy? I love her best of all.'

'I wish she could have stayed,' Bruce replied, and Valerie's heart almost failed her as she looked at his beloved face. 'But her father had that accident so she had to go home, and it seems she changed her mind about Robert.'

Valerie frowned. But Mandy was speaking again and she strained her ears to pick up what was being said.

'You went to the hospital, didn't

you?' Mandy demanded.

'Yes! That's where I saw Valerie and Robert together. I told you about that. Robert had his arm around Valerie. I lost my nerve then and came home.'

'I know Valerie wouldn't go back to Robert,' Mandy said plaintively. 'She told me she didn't love him.'

'But Ruth told me she chatted with Robert last week-end, and he seemed quite optimistic that Valerie would eventually go back to him.'

'You should have spoken to her,' Mandy said tearfully, and Valerie felt as if her heart was being torn in two. 'I miss her! I wish she was here.' Mandy looked up at Bruce and then pointed to what she had written in the sand. 'Is that how to spell her name?' she asked.

'Yes.' Bruce took the stick from Mandy's hand and began to write while Mandy watched intently.

Valerie shook her head, fighting emotion, trying to assimilate what had been said. Bruce had come to the hospital! He'd seen her leaving with

Robert and jumped to the wrong conclusion! But Ruth had said something about talking to Robert! Valerie started nervously when there was a sudden movement at her side and, before she could move, Rajah appeared from nowhere and sprang at her, tail wagging. The dog was delighted to see her, and barked furiously despite Valerie's attempts to quieten him. She had forgotten about Rajah!

Rajah grasped the hem of Valerie's skirt and tried to pull her out of the rocks. She pushed him away, and Rajah turned and ran out to Bruce and Mandy, leaving Valerie breathless but relieved. But the dog seized hold of Mandy's coat and began to tug her towards the rocks. Valerie gasped in horror, and Bruce shouted at the dog.

'Stop that, Rajah. Mandy doesn't want to play games.'

'He wants to show me something in the rocks,' Mandy said. 'What is it Rajah?' She began to walk towards the spot where Valerie was hiding.

Valerie gasped, then shrugged fatalistically, aware that she would have to make the best of the situation. She eased backwards until she could stand and then hurried back a few yards before walking forward as if she had just arrived. She reached the edge of the rocks as Mandy appeared.

'Valerie!' Mandy stared for a moment and then came forward to hurl herself into Valerie's arms. She buried her face in Valerie's neck and burst into tears. 'I knew you'd come back!' she kept repeating.

Bruce was staring at Valerie as if she were a ghost, and she went forward, carrying Mandy, patting her shoulder.

'Hello, Bruce,' she greeted, and he dropped the stick with which he'd been writing in the sand.

Mandy lifted her head and stared at Valerie, tears streaming down her cheeks. But she was laughing. 'It's my eyes again,' she said. 'They're raining, but I'm not crying, 'cos I'm happy.' She hugged Valerie convulsively. 'I knew you'd come back,' she cried.

'I drove down with my father,' Valerie explained, eyes upon Bruce. 'It's his turn to stay at the bungalow.' She kissed Mandy's cheek. 'Why aren't you with Miss Cannell?'

'It's her day off,' Bruce said, 'so I've had Mandy all to myself, which is marvellous.'

'And you haven't been too busy with your plans for the leisure park to take Mandy out?' Valerie enquired.

'The leisure park!' He smiled. 'That's finished, I'm afraid. But it doesn't matter. It served its purpose while I had the dream.'

'Finished?' Valerie frowned. 'Why?'

'I drove to London Sunday night,' he said wearily, 'for a meeting early Monday morning, and all because Ruth was playing what proved to be her last card. She's been twisting my arm, through business, to get me to marry her.' He paused, then added, 'She was a partner in my company.'

'I didn't know that!' Valerie exclaimed.

Bruce smiled. 'Well, I won't go into details. An ultimatum developed on Monday and I challenged it, then discarded the whole leisure park idea to preserve my independence, and to make a clean break with Ruth.' He smiled. 'Of course, when the leisure park went, Ruth went with it.'

'And, since he came back from London, he's had plenty of time for me,' Mandy said excitedly. 'Isn't that great, Valerie? And now you're back, too. We could go out for the day tomorrow.'

'I intended going back to London tomorrow,' Valerie said slowly, and Mandy's arms tightened around her neck in silent protest. 'But under the circumstances I think I could be induced to stay. However I must say that no matter what you heard about Robert and me — we are finished.'

She moved around in order to read what Bruce had written in the sand but he stepped in front of her, his face suddenly serious.

'Before you look at what I've written you'd better tell me one thing,' he challenged.

She smiled. 'Certainly. What is it?'

'Is your expression always perfectly honest?'

'My expression?' She shook her head. 'I don't understand.'

'Your expression told me many times during the two weeks you were here that you had fallen in love with me.' He spoke determinedly. 'I want to know if it was telling the truth or whether you were merely indulging your emotions!'

'You do love him, Valerie, don't you?' Mandy cried, as if willing it to be true. 'Tell Daddy you love him!'

'It is true!' Valerie spoke softly, eyes held by Bruce's strong gaze.

He nodded at her words, relief showing on his face. 'That's fine,' he said. 'Now come and see what I wrote before you appeared.'

Valerie moved around until she could see where Mandy had written 'VALE-RIE' in the sand, and gasped when she saw that Bruce had written 'I LOVE' in front of it, and signed his name beneath. She looked up at him, hugging Mandy tightly, and he put his arms around both of them.

'A nightmare has just ended,' he said softly, and kissed Valerie.

She closed her eyes, saying, 'And a dream has just begun!'

Rajah jumped up around them, barking furiously. A seagull swooped low, calling raucously. The sound of the sea came suddenly to Valerie's ears, and peace entered her heart. She tried to imagine the future and saw a rosy picture of romance and happiness with the man she loved and a girl who needed her . . .

days. The dogs can come too, so they won't feel they've been abandoned. They really are the nicest dogs I've ever met.'

'Oh Adam. You are totally amazing. It really is love me, love my dogs, isn't it?'

'It really is love,' he agreed.

THE END

We do hope that you have enjoyed reading this large print book.

Did you know that all of our titles are available for purchase?

We publish a wide range of high quality large print books including:
Romances, Mysteries, Classics
General Fiction
Non Fiction and Westerns

Special interest titles available in large print are:
The Little Oxford Dictionary
Music Book, Song Book
Hymn Book, Service Book

Also available from us courtesy of Oxford University Press:
Young Readers' Dictionary
(large print edition)
Young Readers' Thesaurus
(large print edition)

For further information or a free brochure, please contact us at:
Ulverscroft Large Print Books Ltd.,
The Green, Bradgate Road, Anstey,
Leicester, LE7 7FU, England.
Tel: (00 44) 0116 236 4325
Fax: (00 44) 0116 234 0205